WINTERBORNE HOME
FOR
VENGEANCE
AND
VALOUR

Also by Ally Carter, for teen readers

WINTERBORNE HOME FOR VENGEANCE AND VALOUR

ALLY CARTER

ORCHARD

ORCHARD BOOKS

First published in the United States in 2020 by Houghton Mifflin
Harcourt Publishing Company
This edition published in Great Britain in 2020
by The Watts Publishing Group

1 3 5 7 9 10 8 6 4 2

Text copyright © Ally Carter, 2020

The moral rights of the author have been asserted.

A CIP catalogue record for this book is available from the British Library.

ISBN: 978 1 40835 737 8

Typeset in Bembo by Avon DataSet Ltd, Bidford-on-Avon,
Warwickshire

Printed and bound in Great Britain by Clays Ltd, Elcograf S.p.A.

The paper and board used in this book
are made from wood from responsible sources.

Orchard Books
An imprint of Hachette Children's Group
Part of The Watts Publishing Group Limited
Carmelite House
50 Victoria Embankment
London EC4Y 0DZ

An Hachette UK Company
www.hachette.co.uk

www.hachettechildrens.co.uk

To Cat, who always had more faith in me
than I had in myself

PROLOGUE

Everybody knows what happened to the Winterbornes – that one day, twenty years ago, two perfect parents took their five perfect children out on their perfect boat for a day upon the water.

Everybody knows that, twelve hours later, only one Winterborne returned – bloody and bruised and clinging to the smouldering rubble, with absolutely no memory of that anything-but-perfect day.

Everybody knows that the lone surviving Winterborne grew up with the finest chefs and governesses. That he had only the best tutors and wore only the nicest clothes and was a charming boy, with his mother's quick wit and his father's kind eyes.

Everybody knows that the young Winterborne heir was destined for greatness – that, despite his tragic past, he had been born a prince and would, surely, someday become a king.

Until the day when Gabriel Winterborne simply walked away from his perfect life, never to return again.

Nobody knows the truth.

THE MUSEUM

'And on the right we have young Gabriel Winterborne!'

April looked to her right, but it was just another painting. In a whole room full of paintings, none of which were all that impressive to April. After all, you can't eat oil-covered canvases. Or, well, you *could*. But April strongly suspected you probably shouldn't. You could burn them for firewood, of course. Maybe sell them down on Front Street to the old woman with the long white braids and the dog that looks like a fox. But there was no point in wondering what a painting like that might be worth. No one like April was ever going to own one.

But that didn't stop the young woman in the burgundy blazer from looking up at the painting like it was the most beautiful thing she'd ever seen.

'Note how Gabriel clings to his father's hand? He was ten when it was painted, and it's the last known portrait of the Winterborne family. A month after it was finished, his whole family would be dead and young Gabriel would be *orphaned*. Can you imagine?' the guide said, but then she seemed to remember who she was talking to. She looked at the kids who filled the room.

Some ran a little too fast. Some stood a little too still. All wore clothes that didn't quite fit, and they looked at those paintings as if they too were wondering how many meals one of them might buy. But Blazer Lady just threw her shoulders back and raised her voice, shouting over the Johnson twins, who were arguing about which superhero's farts would smell the worst.

Because they were at a fancy museum.

They were on their best behaviour.

'Follow me, children! Follow me!'

The museum was super pretty, April had to admit. Nicer than the group home. Cleaner than the school that was only open four days a week because they couldn't afford to run the buses on the fifth day. Which meant on the fifth day, there was no free lunch, which meant on the fifth day, April usually had to be 'creative', but that was OK. Being creative kept April sharp. And, besides, it wasn't going to last for ever. As soon as her mum came back, everything would be OK.

So April decided to enjoy the bright, clean rooms with the shiny wood floors and tall windows. Even the air smelled fancy (fart debates aside). They were close to the ocean, and the breeze was clean and fresh. April felt like maybe she'd climbed on to a spaceship that morning instead of a rusty school bus. It felt a lot like it had brought her to another world.

For reasons April couldn't quite pinpoint, she turned around and took one last look at the steel grey eyes of the Winterbornes.

'Hey, April!' Girl Taylor whispered. Boy Taylor was on the other side of the room, joining in the fart discussion. 'I dare you to touch it.' Girl Taylor pointed at the painting, crossed her arms, and tried to look tough. But April was very good at a number of things; ignoring foolish dares happened to be one of them.

'What's wrong?' Caitlyn with a *C* asked.

'Are you too chicken?' Kaitlyn with a *K* said, chiming in.

'Nope,' April told them. 'Too smart.'

April shouldn't have said it. She was always doing that – letting her inside thoughts become her outside words. It was one of the things she wasn't good at, and it made people like Girl Taylor and the C/Kaitlyns hate her even more than they already did. But April couldn't help the fact that she was different – that foster care was temporary for her. That her mother was coming back – probably any day now.

'You think you're so much better than us.' Girl Taylor's hands were still crossed over her chest, and she was sticking out her lower lip. It was her tough-girl stance, and April knew she was supposed to be intimidated.

She just wasn't very good at that either.

'No,' April said, trying to sound nice and sweet. It wasn't her fault she had the kind of face that looked mad unless it was smiling. And smiling for no reason made April's head hurt.

'I just know what that is.' April pointed to the tiny sensor that was sticking out from behind the painting. 'Laser,' she whispered, like that single word should be explanation enough. But judging from their expressions, it wasn't. 'It'll cut off any finger that touches it.'

'No, it won't.' Caitlyn with a *C*'s voice sounded sure,

but her eyes lacked conviction.

'Of course it will. That particular kind of laser burns at fifteen hundred degrees. It has to cauterise the wound as it slices because the museum can't risk getting blood all over everything.'

'Yeah,' Girl Taylor said. 'That's true.' (*It wasn't true.*) 'I knew that.' (*She totally didn't know that.*)

April forced a smile. 'Of course you did. You probably saw the guards, too.'

'Uh . . . *guard*.' Kaitlyn wasn't that impressed, and she made sure April knew it.

But April pointed to the other side of the room. 'Yeah. One uniform. But that janitor has been cleaning whatever room we happen to be in since we got here. And she's wearing an earpiece identical to the guard's.'

That part really was true. April didn't know how she noticed these things. Or why. Sometimes she thought it must be because her mother was a world-famous art thief. Or spy. Or thriller writer. But whatever made April think the way she did must have come from nature. Her mother hadn't been around long enough for nurture to have had much effect.

Yet.

7

After all, her mother was coming back. Soon.

'Yeah, well, maybe she's not a guard,' Girl Taylor said. 'Maybe she's April's *mother*.'

And just like that, everyone remembered the pecking order. April wasn't the alpha female. She wasn't the beta either. In fact, April wasn't even part of the pack, and that was very much the way she liked it.

'No. I think *that's* April's mother.' Kaitlyn pointed to a painting by Picasso of a woman who was shaped like a Barbie doll that someone had put in the microwave.

'No,' Caitlyn said, catching on to the game. She found a painting of Medusa's severed head being held aloft by a dude with a sword. 'That's April's mother.'

The three of them laughed like they were super funny, and April laughed too. It was easier that way, she'd learnt three group homes ago. Better to fake laugh some of the time than fake smile all of the time. That was just maths.

Besides, the guide was looking at them and yelling, 'Girls! Keep up!'

April didn't know when – or why – the museum had gotten so crowded. Suddenly, it was like the bell had just rung, and there wasn't enough room in the hall as April

8

pushed against the current of people that was flowing in the opposite direction. She might have been lost if she hadn't seen the guide in the centre of the big atrium, looking up at a man who stood a little too tall and a little too still to be human. Which he wasn't, April realised once she got a little closer.

'Now, who can tell me who this is?' the woman asked the kids.

And they all yelled, 'The Sentinel!'

The guide laughed. 'I guess that was an easy one.'

'Go, Sentinels!' Boy Taylor yelled, and the beta boys whooped.

'Yes. Most people know about the mascot, but who can tell me about the *legend?*' the guide asked. For the first time that day, April felt the kids go quiet. Still. They leaned closer, and the woman dropped her voice as she said, 'Two hundred years ago, a ship was crossing the sea when a terrible storm began to brew. The crew knew they had to lower the sails or risk being blown off course, but the sails were stuck, and they wouldn't come down. Lightning struck. The wind roared. And while the captain shouted and the crew panicked, the ship's lookout began to slowly climb the mast, higher and higher, a long knife held between his teeth, and a sword in his belt. He wasn't much more than a boy, but he kept climbing and climbing and then—'

'He cut the sail?' one of the beta boys asked.

'No,' the guide said simply. 'He fell into the ocean and died.'

It was like the air went out of the group – like they'd been holding their breaths and hadn't even realised it.

'But then a great big wave tossed him back on to the ship, and when the crew looked up again, the lookout was high on the mast, cutting the sail free, and saving their lives.'

'So he *didn't* die?' a Johnson twin asked.

The guide raised her hands and shook her head. 'No one knows. They say that, in the next moment, the wind blew and lightning struck, and the captain was never seen again. Eventually, the ship reached land, but for weeks – months – years later, there were reports of a young man wielding a sword and long knife, wandering the city, always there to help when evil was about to strike! Always wearing black. Always disappearing into shadows, like the mist rolling off the sea.'

For a long time a hush descended over the group,

but then the kids began to mumble and whisper amongst themselves.

'The Sentinel's not a legend!'

'Yeah. My grandpa said the Sentinel is real.'

'The Sentinel lives in my old neighbourhood.'

'Man, you're crazy. There ain't no Sentinel.'

'Then how do you explain . . .'

The individual arguments bled together until it was just like the fart discussion, but with a far less obvious answer. (The Hulk. The Hulk's farts smell the worst.)

April didn't want to be part of the argument or the crowd. She just wanted to enjoy the sweet-smelling air and the bright, clean room, so she drifted away from the kids, through the exhibit, and into the big, wide hall, where she found herself standing with a group of adults who all seemed to be waiting for . . . something.

But April had never liked waiting.

WILL THE REAL GABRIEL WINTERBORNE
PLEASE STAND UP?

As April pressed and slipped and weaved and squirmed her way through the crowd, she realised that most of the people were carrying notepads. At least three ladies were holding microphones and wearing too much makeup and standing beside men with big cameras resting on their shoulders.

A silky red ribbon stretched across the doorway – like the finish line of a race – but no one moved towards it, which seemed like a waste to April, but then someone said, 'Ladies and gentlemen, thank you for joining us!' and she saw two men approaching from the other side.

One of them was carrying a comically large pair of scissors and had a look in his eye – like he (A) knew his scissors were ridiculous and (B) would have loved to have been anywhere other than there. But he forced a smile as the first man kept talking.

'As the museum's director, it is my great pleasure to open our newest exhibit – one that I've been working on for quite some time, I don't mind saying.' He laughed and glanced at the man with the supersized scissors and the very sad eyes. 'The Winterborne family has been the cornerstone of our community for more than a hundred years. Building industry. Championing the arts. In fact—'

'Mr Winterborne!' one of the women with the microphones yelled. 'Has anyone claimed the reward?'

It took a moment, but eventually, the man with the scissors shook his head and said, 'No.'

The director looked angry that someone had dared to interrupt his speech. He was just opening his mouth to speak again when another shout came from the crowd.

'Is it true you're going to have your nephew declared dead if no one claims the five million dollars?'

April's eyes went wide. *Five million dollars?* Surely that wasn't right?

But Sad Scissor Man didn't correct them. If anything, he seemed extra sad as he said, 'My nephew has been gone for a decade. I had hoped that a reward for information about his whereabouts would help us locate him, but we've had no success, and so—'

'Uncle Evert?'

The voice was low and gravelly but loud enough to make the man stop. The crowd whirled around and parted, clearing the way as the stranger slipped closer to the red ribbon and the man with the giant scissors.

'Uncle Evert, don't you recognise me? It's me. Gabriel!' the man said. The crowd gasped. And Evert Winterborne looked like he was going to pass out.

But before anything else could happen, another voice rang out from the other side of the room, shouting, 'Imposter!' and the crowd shifted to take in a different man. This one was scruffy and ragged, wearing expensive clothes that had definitely seen better days. '*I* am the real Gabriel Winterborne!' the newcomer shouted.

All around April, cameras started to flash. She heard one of the women with the microphones say, 'Please tell me you're getting this.' The cameraman nodded as Gabriel #1 pushed towards Gabriel #2.

'Liar!' Gabriel #1 shouted and the whole room turned like they were watching a tennis match.

'Imposter!' Gabriel #2 yelled, and April suddenly

14

was afraid she might get dizzy.

'Uncle Evert?' Gabriel #1 was inching towards the red ribbon and the man, who was slowly backing away. 'Surely you know me? I'm Gabriel. I'm your long-lost—'

'Scum!' Gabriel #2 yelled, and April couldn't help but notice that he'd suddenly started speaking with a very bad, very fake British accent. 'You are no Winterborne, sir! I am the true Winterborne heir!'

'Liar!'

'Scoundrel!'

'Imposter!'

'Thief!'

Neither of them looked anything like the boy in the paintings. And it was like neither of them had ever heard of DNA. But five million dollars was on the line. April didn't even have enough money to pay the fines she had at the library.

'Stop!' Sad Scissor Man shouted, and both Gabriels suddenly went quiet. 'My nephew is gone. My nephew is, in all likelihood, dead.' He started to turn and leave, but then he remembered the ginormous scissors and the ribbon and the reason everyone but April was standing around.

15

'Here.' He gave the ribbon a snip. 'Consider the Winterborne Exhibit officially open.'

And then he walked away.

April had no idea what happened to the fake Gabriels. They must have given up and skulked away. Regardless, nobody was paying much attention to her as she drifted past the cut edges of the ribbon and into the big room filled with more paintings and statues. But other things too – like mannequins in long ball gowns and sequin-covered dresses with fringe along the hems. There was a uniform from World War II, and a wedding dress made out of the most delicate lace that April had ever seen.

With every step it was like she went further and further back in time, until she was looking at a sign that said **THE WINTERBORNE FAMILY JEWELS**. Then all April could do was stand there . . . hypnotised. Mesmerised. Staring at necklaces and rings and strings of pearls so long they could have wrapped April up like a mummy.

And that was when she saw the box.

It was about the size and shape of a shoebox, but like no shoebox that April had ever seen. This box was covered in gold and pearls, diamonds and rubies, but the most interesting thing in April's opinion was the lock that sat

16

in the centre of the ornate crest.

An ornate crest that looked exactly like the one on the key that April had worn around her neck every day since she was three years old.

An ornate crest that April had traced with her fingertips, over and over and over again – the only gift from a mother who had left her at a fire station with nothing but that key and a note that read *This is my baby, April. Keep her safe. I'll be back soon.*

That's how April knew that her mother would come back for her. That's how she knew that all the Taylors and C/Kaitlyns in the world were wrong. They had to be!

Ten years in the system had taught April that parents abandon kids, sure. But they don't abandon keys to treasure chests. And April had been looking for her mum ever since.

But as April inched closer and closer to the small ornate box, she couldn't shake the feeling that, all this time, she'd been looking for the wrong thing.

A NIGHT AT THE MUSEUM

April had many talents. At least five. Maybe six, depending on how you counted them.

For starters, she was the best climber at any of the houses she had ever lived. She was the best at freeze tag and the least afraid of spiders. No one ever found her when they played hide-and-seek, and she was the most likely to remember things like what the combination was to the lock they kept on the refrigerator, even if she only saw her foster mother punch it in one time in the dark.

That night, April was grateful for all of her talents.

They were what let her sneak, light as a feather, through the living room and collect a pack of matches, a black hoodie, and a banana (because you should never do a heist on an empty stomach).

She'd paid careful attention at the museum and remembered exactly where the service entrance was and what code the guards had used to go in and out. She'd noticed the gap in the fence – too small for someone who wasn't completely desperate to even think about crawling through.

But, most of all, April was completely desperate.

She was little and she was strong and she had absolutely nothing to lose.

The parking lot was empty when she got there. There were security cameras, of course, but they were the kind that moved, and that only happens if the cameras have blind spots, so April stood perfectly still for a long time, watching the cameras sweep across the dark lot. Really, it was just like dodgeball, and April was excellent at finding the place on the court where no one had an easy shot. Then she slid through the fence and across the parking lot and to the door that opened with a tiny *click*.

Inside, there wasn't even a laser grid. No iron grates. Not even a single German shepherd roaming around, growling up at her as soon as she inched quietly inside.

It was dark, though, so April was glad she'd brought the matches and remembered the silver candelabra that was sitting with the Winterborne family dishes.

It only took a moment for her to light all the candles and then ease through the big, deserted room. Moonlight shone through the windows. The old gowns practically glowed, and April felt her heart beat a little faster. Her hands started to tingle, like her fingers didn't want to work with the rest of her body. Like they knew they were getting ready to touch whatever it was her mother wanted her to find.

The room seemed different in the darkness. Maybe it was all in April's mind, but it smelled different too. Almost like . . . the Hulk's farts. And a gas station parking lot. (Which, really, is kind of the same thing.)

But she moved on until she was standing in front of the little jewel-covered chest. For a moment she just stood in the candles' flickering light, breathing. Watching. She didn't see any sensors. There weren't any cameras on the walls.

There was a giant mirror, though, and when April saw a man behind her, she jumped. But it was just the statue of the Sentinel, standing in the atrium, keeping watch, and she realised that the only other person in the building was either a ghost or a legend, and neither one would be strong enough to keep her from finding out what was in that chest.

April stopped breathing, and her hands started shaking, and the key bit into her palm as she held it. Waiting. Wondering. Hoping and praying just a little.

Was it a letter? A map? Maybe the number for a Swiss bank account or a book at the public library – one that would have a code written on the back page in invisible ink and she'd have to use lemon juice and a hair dryer just to read it?

It was quite possible that this was just the first step. She might just be beginning her quest tonight, but that was OK. At least she'd be on her way.

So she put the key in the lock.

And took a deep breath.

And turned.

And absolutely nothing happened.

'It's stuck,' April said, even though no one was there to hear her. She wiggled. She jiggled. She even spat on the lock, hoping it was just old and rusty and figuring spit had to be good for something.

But the key didn't turn.

Which had to be a mistake.

She looked behind her, searching the room for some kind of solution. The Sentinel still stood in the atrium. A knife in his belt.

She could pry the lid open, April realised, whirling back around. But she'd put the candelabra on the case and hadn't noticed the wobble. She certainly wasn't expecting it to tip.

April absolutely did not intend for all five candles to go tumbling off the side of the case, falling to the floor.

'No!' she shouted, but it was too late. The long white gown had a train of delicate lace that swept all the way to April's feet. She saw the candles land. Immediately, she leapt to kick them out, but the antique lace was like a fuse, and the fire was soon blazing down the train of the wedding dress and up the hem of every garment it passed – jumping from the clothes to the curtains. From the curtains to the wall.

April wasn't sure when the alarms started blaring or the lights started swirling. Really, she wasn't hearing too well. Or seeing too well. Or breathing too well, come to think of it.

She was thinking just well enough to turn back to the little chest and pull out her mother's key.

It was far too late to stop the fire. The room was filling with smoke, and April felt herself stumbling. She had to get to an exit. She had to get outside. She had to get away, but—

She fell.

And the key tumbled from her hand, disappearing among the flames and the smoke and the terror that was stronger than anything that April had ever felt in her life.

There was a little more air down there, of course, and April was mad at herself for forgetting that smoke rises. She started scrambling and clawing, fighting against the smoke and fire and time itself as she ran her fingers along the floor, searching. Desperate.

The smoke was swirling now. The shadows were moving. It was almost like the Sentinel was alive. Like he was with her. Like she didn't have to die alone. She could feel him sweeping closer and closer.

And closer.

And as her vision filled with stars and she drifted off to sleep, one thought filled her mind: *I thought he'd be taller.*

HOW TO TRUST A PERSON WITH
NO STAINS ON THEIR WHITE TROUSERS

April had always been really good at waking up. She never tossed. She never turned. But maybe that's because she never really slept either. A part of her brain was always right there on the edge, teetering. Like she knew that, at any moment, she might have to get up.

And run.

So it was more than a little unusual that she rolled over and tried to go back to sleep. She'd been having a dream where she was flying, swooping through the clouds, weightless above the city.

But something wasn't right, the part of her brain that never really slept tried to tell her.

First of all, the sheets beneath her fingers were too clean. They smelled like bleach and were rough against her fingers. The room was too quiet. Only a steady, rhythmic beeping filled the air – no snoring roommates or barking dogs.

But the biggest thing that kept April from returning to sleep was the pain.

Everything hurt. Her head pounded, and her throat burned. Her hands and arms and legs felt like they'd been put through a meat grinder, and a part of April wanted to go back to sleep just to forget about how much everything ached and itched. Maybe she could have the dream again. It was a good dream, about—

'The Sentinel!' The realisation hit, and April jerked upright in the bed. Which was a mistake. Because sitting up so quickly made her head feel like it was a rubber ball that had been dropped from the very top of a five-storey building. She actually thought she might feel her brain bounce.

But that wasn't the weirdest part.

The weirdest part was that she wasn't alone.

She should have known it – sensed it. Survival meant always knowing when someone was behind you, whether it was a robber or, worse, a Johnson twin. But April was surprised to see a face staring back at her from the chair beside the bed.

'Not quite, no,' the woman said. And April couldn't disagree. This woman didn't look like an urban legend. She looked like a . . . ghost. She had black hair and blue eyes and pale skin. Red lips. Really, she looked like something from an old Disney movie – like maybe she was a princess. Or a witch.

But the thing that caught April's attention the most was that she was dressed, head to toe, entirely in white.

She had on white trousers and a fluffy white sweater and a long coat the colour of brand-new snow.

Maybe she's an angel, April thought.

Maybe I'm dead?

Could I be dead?

Yeah, April thought, remembering the fire. *I could totally be dead.*

But if wearing white was a requirement, April was in trouble because she'd never owned anything white in her life. April got everything dirty.

'Who are you?' she asked, then looked around the room. It was obviously a hospital, but the last thing she remembered was the museum and the smoke and the fire. 'How'd I get here? Am I in trouble? Is there anything to eat? Where . . .' But the words were suddenly too thick and scratchy, and when she started coughing, she didn't think she'd ever stop.

The woman eased a little closer to April's bed and held out a plastic cup with a bendy straw. 'Drink.'

'What is it?' April asked, but the words came out like a croak.

'It's water. Your throat has to hurt.'

April's throat did hurt, so she did as she was told.

The woman crossed one leg over the other and said, 'You were brought here in an ambulance after the firefighters found you last night. Don't you remember?'

April shook her head, then grabbed a container of jelly off the tray on her bedside table. She ripped off the top but didn't even look for a spoon. She just brought the plastic cup to her mouth and sucked. It made a slurping sound, and the Woman in White winced. She wanted to tell April to stop, April could tell. So April slurped harder.

'How do you feel, April? I know this must be scary for you.'

April slurped again. 'You don't know me.'

'I know enough.' Something in the way the woman said it made April think that maybe she did. That maybe she knew more than even April. After all, she knew how to walk around in white trousers without getting even a speck of mud on them. She knew how to keep stains off of her white sweater. Clearly, on some level, this woman was a genius, and April wanted to apprentice in her ways. But, more than anything, April wanted to take care of April. After all, no one else was going to.

'I know you've been in twelve homes in ten years.'

April laughed a little at that, then used her pinkie finger to dig some jelly out of the bottom of the cup.

'I've been in twelve *houses*,' April corrected. She didn't bother to explain the rest of it: that she'd never had a home. 'Are you a social worker or something?'

'Not exactly. But your case agent and I have spoken. She was quite curious about how you ended up where you did. *When* you did.'

'I left something,' April blurted. 'At the museum. I got locked in.'

'Did you leave something, or did you get locked in?' the woman challenged.

April looked her right in the eye and said, 'Both.'

'So that's why you were on the sidewalk last night during the fire?'

April replayed the words in her mind. They sounded like a question. But they weren't, she realised. They were a hint. A clue. This whole thing was a test, and the Woman in White was trying to slip her the right answers.

'Yeah. That's why I was on the *sidewalk*,' April repeated, and the woman nodded slowly. Her blue eyes were like steel. It wasn't an answer. It was a warning.

'The firefighters found you. And an ambulance brought you here.'

The moment stretched out between them. There was nothing but the sound of the beeping machine and the pounding of April's heart until April couldn't take any more and blurted, '*Who are you?*'

'I'm sorry.' The woman laughed. 'My name is Isabella Nelson. I run a charity.'

'I'm not a charity case.' April suddenly felt defensive and sad and so, so sleepy.

She expected an argument. Not for the woman to pick a speck of lint off of her white coat and say, 'That's a pity. We would have liked having you. And I think you would have enjoyed it as well. In fact, your case agent is finalising the paperwork right now, but if you'd rather stay here and answer questions from the police . . .' She trailed off as she started to stand.

'The police?' When April's voice squeaked, she tried to blame it on the smoke damage, but she knew in her heart it was something else.

'Yes. They're most curious to know how the fire started, considering the extent of the damage.'

April swallowed hard and tried not to think about the candelabra. And the way the wedding dress had burst into flames. And the little pack of matches that may or may not have been stuck in her jeans pocket right at that moment, waiting for some surly detective to find it.

'It seems the fire protection mechanisms malfunctioned, and everything in that wing of the museum is gone.'

Gone. The little box was gone – probably just a pile of smoke and ash. She tried to tell herself it didn't matter – that the key hadn't fit that particular lock anyway. The lock April was looking for was still out there! She just had to find it! She just had to . . .

Then April remembered falling. She closed her eyes and watched the key skid across the floor, disappearing into the flames. And then April wanted to cry. She wanted that woman to leave so she could be alone with her tears and the pain in her lungs and her throat and her hand and . . .

April looked down at her hand.

She felt the sharp, familiar pinch that came every time she gripped her key too tightly. And there it was – a little bit blackened, but back on its chain and around her neck exactly where it was supposed to be. Except it wasn't supposed to be there. It should have been a melted pile of goo, but it wasn't, and suddenly it was all too much.

'Where are my clothes?' April didn't know what was happening – or why – but she knew she didn't like it, didn't trust it.

The woman pointed to a bundle on the end of the bed.

'Those aren't mine,' April said.

'Your things smelled like smoke. Plus, they were falling apart and too small already. I think these will be a little more comfortable.'

They aren't white, at least, April thought. They had that going for them.

She stumbled out of the bed, but her legs felt a little wobbly and she had to hold on to the mattress to keep from falling.

'Easy, dear,' the woman said, but April wasn't anyone's dear. Ever. And she didn't let herself think that the Woman in White might mean it. After all, April's mum would

31

be back soon. She'd be somebody's dear then. But in the meantime, it was way more important that April be smart.

'I gotta go,' April said, but to where she didn't know. She just knew that nothing good ever came from waiting, so she pulled the new jeans on under her hospital gown. They were too stiff and the denim was too blue. April had no idea how to wear clothes that had never been worn before, but she buttoned them up anyway because what choice did she have?

'Your case agent will be back soon,' the woman said. 'The doctor said you're well enough to be discharged, but you must realise you can't go back to the group home?'

'Why?' April asked even though she already knew the answer.

'You were found on the street at midnight, a dozen yards away from a museum that was totally engulfed in flames. People have questions, April.'

'So I go to a new house. Whatever. It'll be just like all the others.'

'Not all homes are the same.'

'What do you know about it?' April didn't mean to snap. She certainly didn't want to yell. But there was a little piece of paper poking her in the back of her neck and she didn't want to just rip it out and risk tearing the only new shirt she'd ever owned.

The woman eased around to April's side of the bed then sat down on the rumpled sheets. 'You're right, April. I don't know how it is at other homes. I only know how things are at Winterborne House.'

The woman deftly ripped the tag from April's shirt, but April's mind was back in the museum, looking down on a small chest with a tiny crest. And then April was looking up at the Woman in White, asking, 'Winterborne?'

WHEN THE BITE IS WORSE THAN THE BARK

April had never been in a limousine before. But as soon as she stepped outside the hospital and followed Ms Nelson to the long black car with the windows you couldn't see through, she felt less like she was stepping into a car and more like she was getting into a carriage from a movie. The question remained, though. Was the Woman in White her fairy godmother or her evil stepmother? Only time would tell.

At the moment, she only knew two things for certain:

One: jelly isn't a very satisfying meal.

And two: limousines come with buttons. So. Many. Buttons.

There was one that opened a hole in the roof. One that raised and lowered the divider between the back seat and the driver. There was one for the radio, and one for the lights, and one that opened and closed a refrigerator that held nothing but teeny tiny bottles of water and wet washcloths that were rolled up like burritos.

Man, April really wanted a burrito.

Ms Nelson sat perfectly still on the black leather while April poked and prodded and twisted and turned.

'You need to keep your seat belt on, April,' was her only warning. But she didn't sound mad.

'Um . . . I think I broke something,' April admitted a few minutes later.

'What?'

'I think the car's on fire!' April couldn't believe she'd managed to start *another* fire, but she also couldn't stop twisting and squirming as the leather beneath her got hotter and hotter, but Ms Nelson didn't seem the least bit concerned.

'Yeah. I did it. I started a fire!' April said, but the woman only shook her head.

'No. You just turned on your seat heater.'

'My what?'

'Your seat heater. Here.' She leaned across April and punched a button, and April's rear end began to slowly return to normal.

'So . . . I guess rich people don't like having cold butts, huh?'

'April, *no one* likes having a cold butt.'

When the woman smiled that time, it was a real smile. Not like she was laughing at April. Like they were laughing at something. Together. And for the first time April let herself think that maybe life at Winterborne House wouldn't be so bad.

Maybe?

'So what's your deal?' she said, turning to the woman.

'I apologise. I should have led with that back at the hospital. I'm the director of the Winterborne Foundation. I live at Winterborne House – that's where you'll live too from now on.'

April thought about the museum and all the fancy things that were a pile of smouldering rubble now, thanks to her. Then April thought about the box and the key and the questions that had been with her longer than any fire. 'Is it Winterborne . . . like . . .'

'Like the Winterborne exhibit at the museum?' the woman guessed. 'Yes. And Winterborne Industries. And Winterborne Street. And the Winterborne Metropolitan

Library and . . . Well . . . You get the picture. But the foundation is based out of Winterborne House. Currently. That will be your home now.'

'Why?'

'If you visited the museum yesterday, you must have heard what happened twenty years ago to the Winterborne family.'

'You mean the shipwreck? Yeah. Everyone knows about that.'

The woman shivered a little, and April wondered why she didn't just turn on her seat heater if she was cold.

'You heard about the boy who survived?' the woman asked, and April nodded. 'Well, after the shipwreck, Gabriel lived in Winterborne House all alone. With only the staff . . . and the staff's children . . . for company. Winterborne House was the home of an orphan for a decade. When he went away . . . Well, it seemed a shame for that great big house to sit empty, so the Winterborne Foundation decided to open its doors to kids like Gabriel.'

'I'm not like Gabriel Winterborne.' April didn't mean to sound snotty, but her stomach was growling and her throat still hurt and she couldn't stop thinking about the boy in the painting.

'Not exactly, no.' The woman grinned down at April. 'But you said it yourself, April. You've lived in a lot of houses. I thought you might be ready for a home.'

She folded and refolded her hands, and April found it strange that there was something – anything – that might make this woman nervous.

'Is that because he's dead now?' April blurted, then felt guilty when she saw the woman's face go as white as her coat. 'I mean, maybe he's not dead. Maybe he's gonna come home one day and find a bunch of random kids in his house. What's he gonna say about that?'

The woman smirked at the thought. 'Very bad words – that's what he would say.'

It was almost like she was remembering something and she didn't know whether it should make her laugh or make her cry. So, instead, she looked down at April and said, 'I think you'll like it at Winterborne House. I hope you'll enjoy having a more . . . permanent . . . placement.'

She probably said it to be nice, but April felt the words like a slap. 'I don't need a permanent placement.'

'Everyone does better when they have stability. Everyone—'

'My mum is coming for me. I have a permanent place with her.'

The woman didn't argue. She just tilted her head a little and said, 'Yes, dear. I just meant that you have a place with us for as long as you need it. You'll always have a place with us.'

She patted April's hand and looked out the window. April expected to see a street like the one by the museum. She thought that maybe if she opened the hole in the roof, she might smell the sea. But it was just a regular street with little convenience stores and houses with metal bars over the windows.

'Lady, I hate to break it to you, but I think we might be lost.'

'Not lost,' the woman said as the limo slowed down. 'Just making one more stop.'

They parked in front of a house with a rusty chainlink fence and old plastic toys in the garden, weeds growing up through the wheels.

The woman opened the door and said, 'Please wait here. I won't be a moment.'

And then she stepped out of the dark interior of the limo and into the bright sun.

April wanted to roll down the window and yell for her to be careful, that just about anything in that garden could ruin her white clothes, but before she could even reach for any of the buttons, a terrible sound filled the air.

It wasn't a bark. And it wasn't a growl. It was more like a siren that came in canine form.

April reached for the door, threw it open, and shouted, 'Look out!' just as the biggest, meanest, most slobberiffic dog she'd ever seen came barrelling around the corner of the house, jumping through the weeds like it was a lion and Ms Nelson was a gazelle.

Its teeth were bared, but the woman just stood there. She didn't even step aside or take her white coat out of slobber range before the dog stopped flying and jerked back, landing in the weeds.

That was when April saw the collar and heard the rattling of the chain. There was more growling and barking though, but the woman looked down at the beast and said, 'Enough.'

And, just like that, the dog went silent.

'Shut up, you!' someone else yelled. A screen door slammed. And a woman stepped on to the porch, carrying out the trash. She came down the sidewalk and stopped right in front of Ms Nelson, dropping the plastic bag at her feet.

'This is all her stuff.'

Ms Nelson looked down at the mostly empty sack and said, 'Thank you.'

The stranger crossed her arms and stared at Ms Nelson and all her immaculate perfection.

'You said I'd keep getting the cheque for her.'

'Well, no . . .' Ms Nelson said cautiously.

'Then the deal's off.'

The woman reached for the garbage sack and was starting back for the house when Ms Nelson called, 'We will have to officially transfer Violet into our care, but we're quite willing to compensate you for your trouble out of the foundation's funds.'

The stranger stopped. And turned. 'What's that mean?'

That's when Ms Nelson reached into her pocket and brought out a piece of paper. 'Will this be sufficient?'

Even from the limo, April could see the stranger's eyes go wide before she folded the cheque in half and shoved it down the front of her shirt.

'Yeah. That'll do.'

'Excellent.' Ms Nelson looked around the overgrown lawn. 'Where is she?'

'Girl! Get out here!' the stranger yelled.

For a moment, April wondered if the woman was talking to her. She'd heard words just like those a million times, shouted by people who never even bothered to learn her name. But the screen door screeched again, and someone else stepped on to the porch.

She was younger than April, but it was almost impossible to say by how much. Her shiny black hair was cut short around her face, with a crooked fringe that was too long, almost hiding her big brown eyes. She had the look of frailness that kids get sometimes, like a plant that never got enough water and can't quite reach the sun.

Cautiously, the little girl walked down the rickety steps. The dog barked again, but Ms Nelson said, 'Down,' and it dropped to its belly in the grass even as Ms Nelson knelt down to speak on the little girl's level.

'Hi, Violet! I'm Ms Nelson. I live at Winterborne House. How are you?'

'She don't talk.' The foster mother had a kind of gleam in her eye. Like she'd gotten the woman with the fancy clothes to buy a dud but all sales were final. No takebacks.

But Ms Nelson glanced at the pad of paper that the little girl held in her hands. 'Have you been drawing?' she asked. When the little girl nodded, she turned the pad so that Ms Nelson could see. 'Oh, that's very good. Do you like to draw?'

Violet nodded again.

That was the point where most kids might hide behind their mother's legs, but this little girl didn't have anyone to hide behind. Nothing to protect her from the world except that pad of paper, and Ms Nelson must have sensed it too because when she spoke again her voice was softer.

'Violet, I work at Winterborne House. It's a home and a school, and we'd like it very much if you would come live there. Would you like that?'

April didn't know Violet. But she knew what she was thinking: that Winterborne House might be better than this place, but it also might be worse. The girl couldn't have been older than seven, but she'd already learned that things are more likely to get worse than they are to get better and you're always better off playing the odds.

The foster mother seemed to think this was funny, because she laughed and crossed her arms. 'Good luck getting her to go without her guard dog.'

Ms Nelson rose to her full height but looked down at the dog on the chain. She was just starting to speak when a voice rang out, shouting, 'What's going on here?' and April turned to see a boy walking down the street.

He must have been twelve or thirteen, with light brown hair that probably only got cut once or twice a year and the kind of skin that would burn if he stayed out too long in the sun. The collar of his denim jacket was standing up, not because it made him look tough but because it was warmer that way. But the thing April noticed the most was this: he looked far meaner than the dog. And he didn't have a chain.

In a flash, he was through the gate and the little girl was flying into his arms. He smoothed her hair, and when he spoke again, it was like the words were coming from an entirely different person; they were soft and kind and gentle. 'What's going on, Vi? Did you draw something?'

She nodded but didn't pull away from him long enough to show him the pad of paper that was smashed between their bodies.

When he looked at the woman in the too-clean, too-white clothes, his voice was as sharp as the teeth of the dog. 'Who are you?'

'My name is Isabella Nelson. I'm the director of the Winterborne Foundation. Winterborne House is now a home and school, and we'd like for Violet to come live with us.'

The boy looked from the shiny black car to Ms Nelson's fancy clothes and finally to the little scrap of paper sticking out the top of his foster mother's shirt.

'What's that for?'

The woman stepped back, as if she might be afraid of a twelve-year-old boy. 'They're compensating me for my trouble.'

'She isn't for sale,' the boy growled again.

'I have no wish to buy any child,' Ms Nelson said calmly. 'But it's come to our attention that Violet has a remarkable talent for art, is that correct?' Ms Nelson asked, but she didn't really wait for an answer. 'At Winterborne House we have the resources to help her nurture and develop that talent. And you spent some time in the hospital last fall, didn't you, Violet?'

'She's fine,' the little boy growled, but Ms Nelson cocked her head and studied the boy.

'Asthma can be serious. Especially if unmanaged and untreated. We have a doctor on call at Winterborne House.

Violet would receive the best medical care.' She leaned down as if trying to get Violet to look her in the eye. 'How does that sound, Violet?'

But she was really speaking to the boy, and everyone knew it.

'Whatcha say, Vi?' he asked after a long time, his voice softer as he looked down at the girl, who seemed even younger and smaller than she had a moment before. 'Wanna go for a ride in the fancy car? Move into the big house? I bet they have lots of paper in a place like that?'

Ms Nelson knew a lifeline when she saw one, and she grabbed it. 'Oh yes. We have a whole room just for art!'

The little girl pulled away from the boy. The tears were drying on her face.

Now it was the boy who looked like he wanted to cry. 'That sounds nice, right, Vi? That sounds like a great place to live.' He turned away and April could hear his voice crack. 'I think you'll be real happy there. Just . . . Just send me a picture every now and then, OK?'

Violet knew what was happening before Ms Nelson reached for the little girl – before the boy even let her go. In a flash, she was in Ms Nelson's arms and being carried to the car. Her legs kicked. Her arms reached towards the boy, who wasn't reaching back.

And then a single word broke through the air, 'Tim!'

It was the first word she'd said, and Ms Nelson stopped. It only took a moment for her to consider, then say, 'Tim?'

'What?' he snapped.

'How would you like to come to Winterborne House, too?'

THE HOUSE AT THE EDGE OF THE EARTH

Violet didn't push any of the buttons. Neither did Tim. April thought that probably meant something – but she didn't know what, exactly. She just knew that they sat together, perfectly still, while Tim's arm lay across Violet's shoulders and she looked like she was trying to dissolve into him, even as she kept her gaze on the pad of paper in her lap.

'I apologise, Tim,' Ms Nelson said. 'According to our records, Violet didn't have a brother. We didn't know.'

'I'm not her real brother,' he said, but Ms Nelson smiled.

'Family isn't always something we're born into.'

He didn't smile or speak or do anything but grip Violet a little bit tighter.

'You gonna get in trouble? For taking me?' he asked after a long time.

'Don't worry about that,' Ms Nelson said.

'What are you looking at?'

It took April a moment to realise that Tim was looking at her – talking to her.

'Nothing,' she said too quickly.

Then Ms Nelson shifted and said, 'Tim, Violet, this is April. April's moving to Winterborne House today, too.'

She said it like that ought to make them Best Friends For Ever, but April had met enough kids in the system to know that Tim and Violet got by because they had a lifeboat built for two. April wasn't going to force herself in, risk making it tip over.

'Have you and Violet lived together long?' Ms Nelson asked.

'A while,' Tim said with a shrug. Violet didn't say anything. She just kept drawing on that little pad of paper until, finally, she ripped off the top sheet and handed it to April.

'For me?' April asked. She looked down at the paper and saw a perfect rendition of the emblem on her mother's key. Panicked, April's hand flew to her neck, and she realised that the key had somehow come out from beneath her shirt and was hanging there for all the world to see.

'That's very good,' the woman said as she looked at the picture. 'That's the Winterborne crest. You'll be seeing a great deal of it at your new home. The Winterbornes were wonderful people, but they did go a little overboard with the decorating,' she added like it was a secret, just between the four of them.

Then April felt the car begin to slow and turn. She practically plastered herself to the windows as they pulled through the tallest gates that April had ever seen. The car kept driving, around twisty bends and beneath the branches of tall trees, and then it came to a stop in front of a house that was bigger than the museum. Than the hospital. Than her school and every single house she'd ever lived in put together.

It was made out of dark grey stone and looked almost like a castle. April had to wonder if there were people locked up in any of the tall towers. She thought maybe there might be a moat and a drawbridge. Surely a place like this came with at least one dragon, she thought as she crawled from the back of the car, and out into a wind that smelled like salt and felt like rain.

April could hear the low rumbling sound of the waves. A bright green lawn stretched out to her right but then it seemed to just . . . stop. Disappear. And April looked up at the massive house again, hoping that the wind wasn't strong enough to knock it into the sea.

But Ms Nelson didn't seem concerned at all as she walked towards the big double doors.

'Come along, children. Welcome home.'

Home.

And for some reason, April didn't even try to correct her.

When the doors swung open, a tall slender man in a sleek black suit came out. He had grey hair, rosy cheeks, and a twinkle in his eyes, like a very skinny Santa Claus who'd just shaved off his beard.

'Everyone,' the woman said, 'this is Smithers. Smithers, meet the newest residents of Winterborne House. This is April, Tim and Violet.'

'Hello, Mr Smithers,' April said, because Tim and Violet weren't much for talking.

'No. Just Smithers, dear. He's the butler.'

April wondered for a second if she'd misheard and tried

to run through a list of all the words that rhyme with butler. But . . . well . . . *nothing* rhymes with *butler*, so she felt her eyes get really big.

'At your service, Miss April,' Smithers said with a bow.

April dropped into a curtsy and used her fanciest accent. 'Charmed, I'm sure.'

He looked like maybe he wanted to laugh at her – or maybe *with* her – April wasn't always sure of the difference. And the truth was that April didn't really care.

She was standing on the threshold of a big, scary mansion with a butler and a woman who still hadn't gotten any stains on her white coat. April's life had officially entered uncharted territory, and she didn't know which way to go but forward.

That's the thing about fear, April had learned a long time ago. Sometimes the scariest thing of all is standing still.

'Smithers,' Ms Nelson started, but didn't get to finish because the door was flying open and someone was yelling, 'I'm so glad you're finally here!'

It wasn't until they stepped inside that April saw her: a girl about April's own age. She had dark skin and big brown eyes, and she wore a plaid jumper with the Winterborne crest over the heart. Her hair was in two kinds of balls on the top of her head with tiny red bows at the base of each one.

'Am I going to have to wear bows in my hair?' April whispered to Ms Nelson, but the words were lost against the sound of the girl's voice as she yelled, 'Welcome to Winterborne House!'

The next thing April knew, she was being pulled into a giant hug. Even though April didn't hug. Ever. She didn't even really know how, so she kept her arms straight by her side and just kind of leaned into it. She was pretty sure she was doing it wrong when the girl pulled back and thrust her hand out for April to shake instead.

'Hello,' the girl said, sounding like a tiny businesswoman. 'I'm Sadie Marie Simmons! But you can call me Sadie. Everyone calls me Sadie, so you should too, April. At least I'm assuming you must be April. And you must be . . .' But she trailed off when she saw the boy. 'Who are you?'

'That's Tim,' April said. 'And Violet. She's shy. He's not.'

It took a split second for Sadie to process this new information, but then she just beamed and said, 'Great! Welcome to Winterborne House. I've lived here for ages. Not to brag.' April wasn't sure why that would be bragging, but she didn't think it was the time to say so. 'I'm so glad you're here! I thought I'd give you a tour. If that's OK with you, Ms Nelson?' She looked up at the woman, who nodded.

'That's an excellent idea, Sadie. Do you mind if I tag along?'

'That would be lovely.' The girl turned and said over her shoulder, 'If you'd come with me.'

April was just starting to reconsider her first impression. Surely the girl wasn't twelve. Surely she was thirty. Maybe forty. She spoke exactly like a grownup even if she did skip a little as she started for the stairs.

'Welcome to Winterborne House!' Sadie said again, but louder this time, and the words sounded more formal. Like this was the beginning of a recording that she'd made months ago and someone had just pressed Play.

'Winterborne House was built in 1812 by Reginald Winterborne the First, the patriarch of the Winterborne family.'

There were sweeping stairs and a long hall and a massive oil painting of a man who must have been the patriarch himself.

(April made a mental note to never, ever set it on fire.)

'The house was built in the Chateauesque style out of stone mined from the Winterborne quarry. Over the past two hundred years, it has seen several major additions and renovations and is currently ninety-seven thousand square feet with forty-two bedrooms, sixteen staircases, three dining rooms, a conservatory, and thirty-nine bathrooms, which were added at the end of the First World War.'

'What did they use before then?' April couldn't help but ask.

Sadie shook her head. 'You don't want to know.'

When Sadie said that the house had two miles' worth of stairways and hallways and corridors, April rolled her eyes, but thirty minutes later, she was a believer because her head hurt, her feet hurt, and through the windows, night was starting to fall.

Violet was already yawning by the time they reached the highest floor of the house. April could hear the wind blowing off the sea and feel the cold air soaking through the stones, but Sadie was practically vibrating as she threw open a door and shouted, 'Welcome home!'

April supposed it was a bedroom (because there were beds and all), but it was like no bedroom she'd ever seen before. The beds had tall canopies and matching dressers.

There were paintings on the walls and huge closets full of clothes, and a bathroom with a tub big enough to swim in.

The sun was already down as she walked towards the huge bay window with the wavy glass and plush cushions lining the window seat. The dark glass was like a mirror, and for a moment, April didn't recognise herself in her new clothes in her new room, surrounded by so many new people. It wasn't the first time April had found herself picked up and plunked down in a new house with a new family that wasn't really a family at all. But her hand went to her key, felt its familiar weight, and April knew that this time would be different.

And that was when April saw the rope.

It took her a moment to wonder exactly why it was hanging from the ceiling in the centre of the room, but when Sadie reached for it, she seemed especially excited. Possibly too excited, April realised a little too late, because in the next moment, Sadie was grasping the rope and giving it a massive tug.

Which turned on a ceiling fan.

Which jerked a wire, setting off a mousetrap that someone had stuck to the wall.

Which cut the string that was holding the tennis shoes.

Which dropped to the floor and landed on a skateboard.

Which went zooming to the other side of the room, careening into an iron that tipped over.

And burned the piece of yarn that ran through the pulleys and up to the windows.

Which caused all five window shades to drop in very dramatic fashion, revealing the words:

Welcome!

Home!

April!

And!

Violet!

For a long time, everyone just stood there as if waiting for something else to fall or snap or burn or tip. But when nothing else happened, April began to think that they must have already seen the big finale.

'That was great,' she tried, and Sadie beamed.

'It's one of my own inventions.' She seemed so . . . happy. April had never met a kid quite like her. 'Do you love it?'

Sadie was pointing at the pretty beds with tall canopies and thick velvet curtains you could pull together to make a cosy cocoon. On the other side of the room, there was a fireplace and cushy armchairs surrounded by shelves and shelves of books.

And April had to think hard about her answer.

'This is our room,' Sadie went on. 'Yours and mine and Violet's. Ms Nelson said we should all room together at first because the house is so big and confusing, and we girls have got to stick together. Not you.' She looked at Tim. 'You and Colin will have a different room. No boys allowed!'

Sadie laughed then, but April was walking towards the bed. She looked up at the canopy overhead – at the Winterborne crest that was there, looking exactly like the key around her neck.

'Yeah, Sadie,' April had to say. 'It's perfect.'

THE MIDNIGHT MISSION

April woke up because of the thunder. Or maybe the wind. She wasn't really sure what had pulled her from her dream, except the windows were rattling and a storm was howling, and a little body was shivering beside her, even though the bed was snug and warm.

By April's way of thinking, the big house had been OK since 1812. Not even April's luck was bad enough to make it collapse her first night there. But when the lightning cracked outside and a tree limb blew against the window, the little girl whimpered and snuggled closer, and April said, 'Shhh. It's OK, Violet. Go to sleep.'

But April didn't even try to do the same. How could she when the Winterborne crest was on the canopy overhead, mocking her? Tempting her. So when Violet's breathing became deep and steady, April slipped out of bed and headed for the door.

The key was heavy around her neck, and she had a lock to find. Also, Smithers might have brought them a tray with sandwiches and lemonade earlier, but April had a strong suspicion there might be ice cream in the kitchen.

And April had a policy of never, ever missing ice cream.

The house that had been slightly creepy in the broad light of day was downright eerie in the middle of the night. In the middle of a storm. On the side of a cliff at the edge of the world. At least that's the way April felt as she crept out the door, stepping over Sadie's 'alarm clock' (which was really just an hourglass, a Slinky, a cowbell and an overstuffed sock filled with marbles).

So April was extra double careful as she eased out into the deserted hall. She wished she'd thought to put on some shoes, but cold feet were nothing compared to an empty stomach, and April liked the idea of getting the lay of the land at a time when there would be no kids, no butlers and no women who never got dirty.

Soon, the rain was falling so hard against the windows it was like the whole building was being sprayed with a firehose. Lightning crashed and thunder boomed and

April had the feeling that the ocean was angry.

But April wasn't afraid.

After all, houses can't hurt you. People can, but only if you let them, and April wasn't going to make that mistake again, so she wasn't afraid – even when the little hairs on the back of her neck started to stand on end, telling her that she wasn't alone.

'Who's there?' she called into the darkness, but the darkness didn't answer.

'It's April,' she called again, but only the wind replied.

When April reached the stairs, lightning crashed, too bright, through the windows. The wind roared like sirens, and April watched the shadows dance, knowing she'd seen it all before. She'd felt it all before. And there was only one word on April's mind as she made it to the first floor: *Sentinel*.

She remembered what the kids at the museum had said – that the Sentinel was real, and now April had no doubt.

The Sentinel was down there.

She spun as she felt the air move at her back. She whirled when the floors creaked on the far side of the hall. She almost flew back up the stairs when the lightning struck, sending a wave of white light through the big windows. Then a crash sounded behind her – like the lightning was coming from *inside* the house – and she spun again, staring through the darkness.

Maybe her eyes were playing tricks on her.

Maybe the Sentinel *wasn't* there. But she definitely wasn't alone. She wanted to run away or scream for help. But someone had carried her out of the fire and put her mother's key back around her neck.

Maybe some urban legends wanted to be friends?

'Hello?' she asked the darkness.

She didn't actually think the darkness would talk back.

'There you are.'

'What are you doing here?'

Tim's voice was low, and April understood why that mean woman had called him Violet's guard dog, because April half expected him to growl as he stood on the stairs, looking down at April and her bare feet.

'I live here?' She didn't need Tim's permission for walking around. She didn't need anyone's permission.

And she was just starting to tell him so when he snapped, 'Violet woke up screaming, and you weren't there.'

Just as he finished, there was a crash of thunder and a bright burst of lightning, and the mansion felt like maybe it actually was going to fall into the sea, but April had other problems at that moment, thank you very much.

'She was sound asleep when I left. She was fine.'

'She's not fine!' Tim didn't look twelve. He looked twenty. And like the weight of the world was on his shoulders, like they couldn't possibly grow fast enough to keep up.

'But she's OK now, right? Or else you wouldn't be here?'

It seemed like a valid point, but Tim doubled down.

'She was terrified.'

April wanted to tell him that everyone was terrified sometimes. That not having anyone who cares when you wake up screaming is really just life and everyone has to handle it eventually. But for some reason, she asked, 'So how sick is she?'

'She's fine,' he snapped.

'She was in the hospital, though, right? Is that why you're down here yelling at me?'

'She . . . she has trouble breathing sometimes. I don't expect you to care or anything, but—'

'I care,' April said, and she watched his face shift from anger to something that looked a lot like guilt.

'Yeah. Well, you'd be the first.'

'You care,' April reminded him. 'How long has she been sick?'

'I don't know.' Tim shook his head. 'She was like that when she came to the last house. I came home from school one day, and there was this little girl I'd never seen before, lying on the bathroom floor, trying to breathe.'

'How many homes has she been in? What happened to her parents? Where—'

'I don't know!' he snapped, then looked like he felt bad about it. He looked like he felt bad about everything. 'I'm not her real brother. I'm just all she has.'

Tim didn't say the rest of it – that Violet was all he had, too.

April thought about what Ms Nelson had said in the car, about how some families are the ones you choose. No one had ever chosen April, but she was OK with that. After all, April's mum would be back soon.

'Look, the thing about me is that I'm not going to be here for ever. I want to help Violet, but my mum is coming back for me.' April said it like it was a secret, like she didn't want it getting out because then all the other kids would feel bad, and kids like Tim and Violet had enough things making them feel bad already.

'Oh. Is that right?' Tim crossed his arms and looked down at her.

'Yeah,' April said. 'So I don't want her getting attached . . . OK? I don't want her to be hurt when my mum comes to get me.'

'Yeah. Right. OK,' Tim said. 'So, when *is* your mum coming, exactly?'

'Soon.' April didn't sound defensive. She didn't have to. She was just telling the truth.

'And how long have you been saying that?'

The lightning struck again, and a fresh wave of rain pounded against the windows, and April didn't let herself think about the answer.

'Look,' Tim said, 'I'm not going to get dependent on you. And neither is Violet. Vi and me, we're OK. We'd run away if we had to. But we don't have to, and I know you're not going to be in the system long because your mum is coming back and all, but this is the best place I've ever been. It's the best place Violet could ever be. So Violet and me, we're gonna stick around here. And we're not getting kicked out because of you.'

April didn't want to get anyone kicked out. She just wanted to track down the lock and find her mother and maybe grab some ice cream. She didn't ask for Tim to come yell at her. She didn't ask for anything! So she snapped, 'Then by all means, go back to bed. Don't let me stop you!'

'I won't!' Tim shouted. 'And don't worry. Violet won't be bothering you any more. People who don't talk a lot listen. And Violet's smart enough to know who she can count on.'

He didn't even look back as he started up the stairs, disappearing like . . .

'*The Sentinel.*' April remembered the movement in the darkness and the sinking suspicion that she wasn't alone. She whirled around and studied the shadows. But surely she was wrong, she thought. Surely—

'Ow!' April took a step and felt a piercing stab at the bottom of her big toe. Then another. When she dropped into a chair, she saw blood covering the bottom of her foot and a tiny shard sticking out from the soft skin. April winced as she pulled it free. Then she realised the floor was littered with more pieces – hundreds of them. Larger shards of a broken vase lay in the centre, and April remembered the crash she'd heard just before Tim appeared at the top of the stairs.

Sure, ghosts and urban legends might wander around museums and creepy old houses, but they didn't break things, April knew.

People break things.

In April's experience, people break everything.

THE CALM AFTER THE STORM

The following morning, at seven a.m. precisely, Sadie's hourglass tipped over, causing a marble to become unbalanced and roll down a length of tubing, knocking over a bottle of water that poured out on to a piece of paper, which quickly dissolved, causing the spring-loaded cords attached to the bed curtains to retract quickly, flooding April's bed with the kind of bright, clear sunshine that only comes after a storm.

'Do you love it?' Sadie's face was inches away from April's nose. 'It's—'

'One of your own inventions?' April guessed as she pushed herself upright and looked around.

Sadie was already dressed, and she bounced up and down on the balls of her feet, saying, 'It's your first day! Are you excited? You should be excited. I'm so excited. Aren't you?'

'*Soooo excited*,' April lied, because in truth, all April wanted to do was go back to sleep. She'd been having a wonderful dream where she'd found a second jewelled box and this time the key fit. She was just about to throw open the lid and reveal all the treasure, but now April would never know how it was supposed to end.

'You're going to have such a good day,' Sadie told her. 'Smithers is going to give you *tests!*'

For a moment, April was absolutely certain she'd misheard her. But, no, Sadie was practically vibrating with glee. And envy.

'You'll get assessed on everything – reading, maths, science. How's your French?' Sadie asked, deadly serious.

'I'm fluent in *fry*,' April told her, and it took Sadie a moment to realise April was joking.

'You'll do great,' Sadie said. 'Don't be nervous.'

'I'm not,' April said, and Sadie stopped smiling.

'Oh. Well, maybe be a little bit nervous.'

And after that, April was.

Sadie had to rush off to the kitchen because she had a big surprise planned for breakfast (Sadie's words). Violet was already gone – probably off somewhere with Tim – which left April to make her way downstairs alone. Which was exactly how April liked it.

On some level, April knew that the key wasn't still hot from the fire. But it felt like it was. She could feel it underneath her shirt, burning her skin and making her sweat. She wondered if it might leave a scar. But, honestly, April would have been OK with that. She would have been OK with anything if it brought her one step closer to her mother.

And she was getting closer – she had to be! After all, April had a key with the Winterborne crest, and she was now living in a whole mansion full of Winterborne crests!

April had a key. Which meant that all April needed was a lock.

But Sadie had said that Winterborne House was thousands of square feet, so April needed some kind of plan. A strategy. A blueprint and a list. Maybe Smithers had an archive of all the locked things in the mansion? But he probably wouldn't give it to her unless he was hypnotised or something.

(Note to self: research butler hypnotisation.)

Really, April was starting to think that maybe she was just going to have to search every room on every floor until she either found what her key opened or died of old age. Whichever came first.

So April headed for the first floor because that seemed an obvious place to start. She was halfway down the stairs when she heard it.

'I wouldn't go down there if I were you.'

The voice was small. And close. And had a funny-sounding accent that April couldn't quite place. For a second, it seemed like maybe the people in the paintings were talking, but April wasn't frightened. She was just confused as she stood in the wide, dim hallway and said, 'Hello?'

'You must be the new girl. Or one of 'em, I reckon. Well, don't let me stop you, love, if you want to go down, but take my word for it, you can see better from up here.'

'Um . . . who are you?' April looked around. 'And . . . um . . . *where* are you?'

Then the voice laughed. 'I'm up here. On the floor,' it said, which didn't make even a little bit of sense to April, but as she inched towards the curving staircase and looked up, she saw a boy lying on his stomach, looking through the banister at the foyer down below.

Without realising it, April started to climb, moving slowly on the old steps.

'I'm Colin. And you're April, I'm guessing,' the boy said with a wink. 'Welcome to Winterborne House.'

Then he rolled back on to his stomach and peered through the banister. April wasn't really thinking as she dropped to the soft, plush carpet beside him.

'Where are you from?'

'All 'round. But me mum's from London. That's why I talk funny. Except where I'm from, you'd be the funny-talking one now, wouldn't ya?'

April supposed he had a point. But the most interesting thing about Colin wasn't that he had an accent. No. It was that he also had a mother.

She actually looked around, as if expecting the woman to show up at any moment, but he turned back to the foyer and the door.

'What are you doing?'

'Watching,' he said. 'And waiting.'

'For what?' April asked.

'Haven't you heard?' he asked, his eyes getting wide. 'They've found Gabriel Winterborne.'

9

THE FUTURE MRS WINTERBORNE

April didn't quite know what to think or feel or believe. She just knew that Colin was keeping his gaze trained on the foyer and he was . . . laughing?

'Bet you ten quid this one says he's in the Alps. They love saying that. I guess they figure he'll have a beard and make his own clothes out of animals he's killed or something. So Alps are the odds-on favourite. But they also love small islands in the South Pacific. Sadie has a fiver riding on the islands. What do you think?'

'What do I think about what?' April asked because, really, she wasn't sure what she thought about anything by that point. Almost dying in a fire, getting saved by an urban legend, and going to live in the home of a presumed-dead billionaire would do that to a girl.

'What do you think she's gonna say?' Colin asked.

'What is *who* going to say?' April asked, but then there was the clicking of shoes on the floor in the foyer below. Smithers's back seemed especially straight as he opened the door and ushered a young woman inside.

'*Her*,' Colin said with a grin.

The new woman and Smithers spoke in words too low for April to hear. When Smithers led the woman away, Colin pushed up from the floor and whispered, 'Come on.'

Then he bolted up the stairs and down the hall and through a sliding door that April hadn't even realised was a door at all. For a moment, she stood on the threshold, trying to let her eyes adjust to the dim light while Colin bobbed and weaved among stacks and stacks of—

'Ow!' April stubbed her toe and heard something fall to the floor.

'Shh,' Colin whispered. 'Hurry up. You're missing it.'

Books. April was surrounded by books. Her eyes adjusted to the darkness, and she eased towards the light and the outline of the boy, who was lying on his stomach again, looking down at the library below.

'I'm Gabriel Winterborne's fiancée,' said the stranger. She was pretty, April had to give her that. But she was dressed like someone who had googled *billionaire's girlfriend* and just bought everything that came up. Glitzy earrings. Leather gloves. Tall boots.

'Is that right? Well, congratulations,' Ms Nelson said, but her smile didn't quite reach her eyes.

'He said that if anything should ever happen to him, I should come here.'

'*Did* something happen to Gabriel?' Ms Nelson asked.

April thought that was a perfectly reasonable question, but the fiancée bristled and looked Ms Nelson up and down.

'Who are you?' The stranger sounded annoyed.

'I'm Isabella Nelson, the director of the Winterborne Foundation.'

'Then I believe that's *Mr Winterborne* to you.' The woman actually looked down her nose at Ms Nelson, and Colin laughed.

'Ooh. She'll be regretting that, she will.'

Smithers stepped forward then. 'May I offer you tea, madam? Or coffee?'

'No, Smithers. It is Smithers, isn't it?' she asked. Then

76

she smiled. 'It seems like I know you. Gabriel speaks of you so often. No.' Her voice cracked. '*Spoke.*'

'Not bad,' Colin said, but April could tell that Ms Nelson wasn't impressed.

She asked, 'Where did you meet . . . uh . . . *Mr* Winterborne?'

'Gimmelwald? Do you know it?' the woman said. 'It's a small village in the Swiss Alps. Gabriel had a cabin nearby.'

'Told you,' Colin whispered, but he didn't even glance in April's direction.

'*Had*, you say?' Ms Nelson said.

'Yes. Well . . .' Then there was a handkerchief in the woman's hand and she was walking towards the windows. When she spoke again, her voice was so soft that April barely heard it. 'There was a terrible storm—'

'What's the meaning of this?' It took April a moment to recognise Evert Winterborne without his giant scissors, but there he was, striding into the library like he owned the place. And maybe he did.

'Hello, Evert,' Ms Nelson said. 'It seems Gabriel has a fiancée. A new one.'

The stranger recoiled a little, and April watched her realise that maybe she wasn't the first fiancée who had

77

shown up since Gabriel went missing. But she didn't bother trying to convince Ms Nelson.

'She'll go for the men, you watch,' Colin whispered, and sure enough, the stranger rushed to the uncle, tears in her eyes.

'Oh, Uncle Evert! We have to find him!'

But Uncle Evert simply asked, 'Gabriel Winterborne has a birthmark. Where is it?'

'His arm,' she said after a moment and pointed to a place just above the bend of her left elbow.

'My nephew is allergic to what food?'

'Asparagus,' the woman said, finally getting the hang of the game.

'Where did you meet?'

'At an inn. I was passing through. He'd come for supplies.'

'I see,' the uncle said. 'When was this?'

'Two years ago. We fell in love.'

'And you've been together ever since?'

'That's what people do when they're in love.' The stranger gave a haughty look in Ms Nelson's direction.

'But you don't know where he is now?' the uncle asked.

'We were separated in a storm. But he said if anything ever happened to him I was supposed to come here – that his family would take care of me.'

'Does this happen a lot?' April whispered and Colin shrugged.

'Every couple of months. This one's pretty good. Most never make it past the guardhouse. Evert needs to get a new question, though. Anyone who's ever googled *Gabriel Winterborne shirtless* knows about that birthmark. Not much test for a grifter. And she's a fair grifter.' He gestured to the woman below.

'Maybe she *does* know him,' April said.

But Colin looked at her and tilted his head. 'Aww. You're sweet,' he said, even though April didn't feel sweet. At all. And she was just about to say so when Colin said, 'At least this one didn't bring a kid.'

'They do that?'

'Sure they do,' Colin said. 'Oldest grift in the world. Course, these days, it won't stand up, with DNA and all, but DNA takes time, don't it? And if you've got a family who wants someone back real bad, sometimes you can dangle 'em on for a few days. At least a good grifter can. And she's good.' He gestured to the woman, then shrugged. 'But I've seen better.'

Something in the way he said it, April had no doubt he had. Down below, Smithers was guiding the newest future Mrs Winterborne to the door, but April couldn't take her eyes away from the boy beside her.

'Colin?' she asked slowly. 'Who's the best grifter you ever saw?'

He took a deep breath, and when he spoke again, the words were soft and low. 'One woman came here about a year ago. Dressed real normal, see. No rags. No furs. Just a pretty lady with a boy who looks like the dead guy. That's the key. That and knowing what people *want* to see. And hear. That one they asked to stay awhile.'

'What happened to her?' April asked.

'She ran off. Cleaned out the silver and the safe and was gone by morning.'

'What happened to the boy?'

Colin grinned. And shrugged. And said, 'Nice to meet you.'

'Colin!' Ms Nelson's voice echoed up from the floor below. 'I'm assuming you're up there.'

He scooted closer to the light and the railing, and

yelled, 'She was good, wasn't she? But not good enough.'

'No. She wasn't good enough. Come on, now. You too, April,' Ms Nelson said. 'I'm starving.'

THE SADIEMATIC SEVEN!

April wasn't sure what she was expecting when Colin led her downstairs to the kitchen. Shiny copper pots hung from hooks in the ceiling. The countertops were stone and looked so clean you could eat off them. A funny-looking stove was at the end of the room, and April got the feeling that no matter how much the wind might blow and howl outside, this room would always be warm and cosy and smell like fresh-baked bread. It was instantly April's favourite room that she had ever been in. When she saw the huge window seat lined with fluffy pillows, she wanted to ask if she could just sleep there instead of in her big bed upstairs. April never, ever wanted to leave.

A worn and weathered table sat at the other end of the

room, and that's where Colin led her. It was already covered with bacon and eggs and big heavy plates. It seemed like the kind of table where you wouldn't get in trouble if you spilled. Maybe that's why April wasn't nervous as she slid into a chair so close to the hot butter rolls she could have leaned over and licked the butter off of one if she'd wanted to. Which she *did* want to. But she resisted the urge, and for that she thought she might deserve some kind of medal.

'There you are!' Sadie exclaimed as Colin took a seat. 'I've been waiting for ever. What happened?'

But before Colin could answer, the doors swung open and Ms Nelson came in, Tim and Violet trailing dutifully behind.

'I'm sorry we're late, Sadie. It seems Gabriel Winterborne has a fiancée. *Again*,' Ms Nelson said.

Sadie wheeled on Colin. 'And?'

He smirked and raised an eyebrow. 'Alps.'

'Darn it!' Sadie pulled a five-dollar bill from her pocket and slapped it into Colin's hand.

'Nice doing business with ya.' He slid the bill into his pocket.

'Everyone hungry?' Smithers asked, and April realised

he must have been working on the other side of the room. He carried a huge ceramic dish very, very carefully towards the table. April wasn't sure what was inside, but it smelled like heaven.

Ms Nelson turned to the boy at the other end of the table. 'So, Tim, have you settled in OK?'

'Yeah. I mean yes. Thank you.' He kept glancing at Violet out of the corner of his eye, but Violet wasn't looking at Tim at all. She was too focused on Colin, who was pointing both of his fists in her direction. She'd tap him on the back of the hand, and he'd turn that hand over – lightning fast – and show her his empty palm. Then she'd touch him again, and this time a scrap of paper would be there, like magic.

Violet was laughing, and Tim was looking at her like he'd never heard her make that sound before, and Sadie was standing by the huge oven, a bright smile on her face.

'You have a seat, Smithers,' Sadie announced.

'If you insist,' he said, and made a show of slipping into one of the empty seats at the table while Sadie kept standing.

'Today, ladies and gentlemen,' Sadie went on, standing a little taller and speaking a little louder than she really had to, 'I am pleased to unveil — for the first time ever — the SadieMatic Seven!'

April thought maybe she was supposed to clap, but Colin leaned towards her and whispered, 'You don't want to know what happened to SadieMatics One through Six.'

'This is very exciting, Sadie,' Ms Nelson said, but April noticed that she scooted back from the table a little and Smithers kept glancing at the fire extinguisher that was mounted by the door.

'Everyone ready?' Sadie asked.

'Maybe we should enjoy our breakfast while it's hot,' Ms Nelson said.

'Oh, but this is part of breakfast. See?' And then Sadie pulled a lever that April hadn't noticed before. Soon, the oven door opened and a cookie sheet slid out. There was a large stack of pancakes on it, and April watched, mesmerised, as the cookie sheet was pulled along a track and on to the clean stone countertop beside the stove.

Ms Nelson applauded, and Smithers said, 'Well done, Sadie,' but Sadie *shushed* them and said, 'That's not all!'

'Oh boy,' Ms Nelson whispered.

April noticed a chain that was running along the

ceiling, from the rack holding the pots to the light fixture over the table. A dozen spatulas were working their way through the air. When they reached the place just above the pancakes, a spatula would drop down and pick up a pancake and carry it slowly through the air towards the table.

'Oh, very nice,' Ms Nelson said.

'Now Smithers doesn't have to get up when he forgets things in the oven,' Sadie announced.

'Very handy indeed,' Smithers said, and it was perhaps the strangest conversation that April had ever witnessed. They were being so . . . *nice*. And April couldn't imagine what was in it for them.

'Now, eat up while it's hot, everyone,' Smithers said, and April grabbed a roll. Then another. Then a third just for good measure. They were the warmest, softest, butteriest things she'd ever touched, and she sat there with her eyes closed for a moment, soaking them in.

And maybe that's why she didn't duck.

'Look out!' Colin screamed, but the words were lost amid the sound of shattering glass. Orange juice exploded all over the table.

April looked up just in time to see a pancake hurtling

in her direction. Luckily it missed her, but it hit the table and bounced, taking out Colin's water and knocking over the scrambled eggs. Everyone froze as the big ceramic bowl that was, evidently, full of porridge was hit by a third rogue pancake, tipping it over and sending it flying through the air.

'April!' Ms Nelson yelled, but it was too late. Steaming porridge was already heading towards April like a wave. She tried to duck. She tried to run. But it was like the most delicious tsunami ever, and April could do nothing but stand her ground as it washed over her, drenching and staining her new clothes and turning the buttery rolls in her hands into a soggy mess.

The chain had got tangled among the pots and pans, and the harder it worked to pull free, the harder the pancakes flew across the room, knocking over glasses of orange juice and cups of coffee.

'April!' Ms Nelson raced to April's side. 'Are you OK? Are you burned?'

'No,' April said, even though she thought she might cry because her rolls were covered with porridge. April took a bite out of one to see if it was still edible. And then, for good measure, she ate the entire thing. 'I'm OK,' she said with her mouth full.

'Are you sure you're not burned?' Ms Nelson sounded like she really cared about the answer. Smithers brought a wet rag, and the woman began wiping hot porridge off of April's face and arms.

'It's OK. I've been burned worse,' she said, taking a bite out of roll number two.

'You have?' The woman's voice sounded funny.

'Sure. I mean, burns only count if they blister, right?' That had been the rule in pretty much every house that April could remember, but judging by the way Smithers and Ms Nelson looked at each other, she got the feeling that they might have different rules here.

'Go upstairs and take a cool shower, sweetheart. And then I'll bring you a tray if you're hungry.'

But April had found that the rolls *were* still perfectly edible, so she ate the third one. She might have grabbed a fourth, but everyone was looking at her and April hated being looked at, so she pushed away from the table. She was walking towards the door when she noticed Sadie.

'It didn't work.' Sadie's lip was quivering, and tears were in her eyes, and April didn't know what to say.

'There's some room for improvement,' Ms Nelson told her. 'But, look, we didn't even need the fire extinguisher.'

'So . . . what . . . you're saying is . . . they're getting better?' Sadie sputtered even though April didn't think Ms Nelson was saying that. At All. But the woman smiled and pulled Sadie into her arms.

For a moment, April wondered what that felt like, but she couldn't start to guess.

Maybe it was the way the warm porridge was starting to seep through her clothes or the knowledge that everyone in the house was now ensconced in the warm kitchen without her, but Winterborne House seemed especially cold as April made her way to the big main stairs.

Not all of the Winterborne family artwork must have been lost in the museum fire, because there were portraits on the walls. Silver eyes stared back at her, and she thought she saw them moving, following her every step. She could have sworn she wasn't alone. Except that was crazy. *Or maybe not*, April thought when she turned the corner and found a man in a three-piece suit staring at a wall as if it were the most interesting thing in the world.

'Uh . . . hello?' April said, and the man jolted at the sound of her voice.

'Hello,' he said, eyeing April in all her porridge-covered glory. 'I'm Evert Winterborne. And who might you be?'

'April.'

'April what?' Evert asked.

'I don't know.'

Her confusion must have shown on her face because he said, 'What's your *family* name?'

'I don't know that either.' April still didn't understand the question. She didn't have a family. Or if she did, she sure didn't know what their name was.

'I see. And how long have you been at Winterborne House?'

'I don't know,' April said again. 'What time is it?'

She didn't mean it to be funny, but he must have thought it was because he laughed, but it didn't match his sad eyes. April had seen him in the library with the fake fiancée and Smithers and Ms Nelson. She'd thought he must have left, but maybe he just knew what to expect from the SadieMatic Seven, because he was staring at her filthy hair and porridge-drenched clothes as if April herself was a stain on his family home.

'I spilled,' she said as if that should explain it all.

The house moaned and the wind howled, but Evert just stood there, staring at her as if she was the one who was intruding.

'You were at the museum,' she said. 'I mean, I saw you there. Do you have to bring your own big scissors to those things? And where do you get scissors that big? Do you ever use them for anything else? If I had giant scissors, I'd probably use them all the time. Just for fun, you know? Can you imagine pulling them out on the first day of school?' April was rambling, but she couldn't make herself stop. 'Whatcha doing here?' she asked because, really, someone else was in control of her tongue at that point. April certainly wasn't.

'I'm *Mr* Winterborne. This is my home. I was raised here.' He puffed out his chest just a little and drew a deep breath, like he was fighting against the words he really wanted to say. He ran a hand lovingly along the wood, almost like he was looking for . . . something. 'This house is . . . shall we say . . . a treasure.'

'Do you live here?'

'No, April. He doesn't.' Ms Nelson was walking up behind April, saying, 'Evert, I didn't realise you were still here, or I would have invited you to breakfast. There was porridge.'

'I see that.' He took a long look at April. 'I was just leaving.'

'I'll walk you out,' Ms Nelson said before glancing back at April. 'Go on, dear. It's OK.'

But April had her doubts. She couldn't help it. Having doubts had kept her alive so far, and she really didn't see any reason to change now.

GETTING SCHOOLED

Turns out, Sadie hadn't given them the full tour the day before.

'I had to save something for day two!' she exclaimed as she led them up the third flight of stairs, higher and higher and further and further away from Smithers and his warm kitchen.

When they moved down a long hall at the back of the house, April could practically feel the wind as it blew off the sea, cutting through the old, wavy windows. With every step, her breath came harder and the key around her neck felt heavier. Searching every room of Winterborne House was going to take for ever. And ever. And a day. April would be as old as Smithers by the time she found whatever her key fit. Unless she got lucky.

And April was never, ever lucky.

So she huffed along in Sadie's wake, trying not to let her worry show.

'Sadie,' Tim asked, 'just how much of Winterborne House did you save?'

'Not much,' Sadie replied. 'Just the very . . .' She stopped at the end of the hall. 'Best!' She reached for a pair of double doors. 'Part!' She threw open the doors and held her arms out in the universal signal for *ta-da!*

At first, April wasn't sure what she was looking at.

It wasn't the library – though there were books. And it wasn't a bedroom – though there were cushions and pillows and a pair of cosy chairs in front of frost-covered windows with a clear view of the sea.

But there were other things, too. A big square table and small desks. There were posters on the walls and an old-fashioned blackboard on wheels that someone could ride like a skateboard if they wanted to. Which, obviously, April *did* want to, but she knew better than to try.

'What is this place?' Tim asked, and April was glad she didn't have to.

'It used to be the nursery and governess quarters,

94

back in old-timey days. Now it's the classroom,' Colin told them.

'And it's where I do my experiments!' Sadie looked like her eyes were going to turn into little hearts but then she noticed a glass beaker in the corner was starting to smoke. 'Ooh. It's ready,' she said, reaching for a thick pair of gloves and some plastic safety goggles while Tim pulled Violet behind him. Just to be safe.

'You don't have to worry about her,' Colin told them softly. 'Smithers keeps the dangerous stuff locked up in an unknown location after . . .'

'The SadieMatic Four.' Sadie gave a deep sigh and hung her head. 'It was so great in theory.'

Colin settled down with a laptop while Tim and Violet went to draw on the board. Sadie was utterly consumed with her experiment, which left April on her own in the big room full of other people.

She wandered to the wall between the windows. There were shelves with old textbooks and plastic body parts and a brightly coloured model of something that looked very scientific.

Tucked in beside the model was a photograph. It had a thick white border and a grainy image, but there was no mistaking the little boy in the picture. He had dark hair and silver eyes and looked to be about April's own age as he stood between a girl and a man who was holding up a smoking beaker in a way that was entirely too familiar.

'That's my dad.' April jumped at the sound of Sadie's voice.

She wasn't sure what surprised her more – Sadie's words or her tone. It was the first time April had seen her not bouncing. But she wasn't sad either. She was just . . . normal. Or like a normal girl in April's world.

'He worked at Winterborne Industries,' Sadie said. 'He was an inventor. A really, really good one. Then, after the accident, when Gabriel needed a tutor . . .' Sadie trailed off, as if the rest of the story told itself. 'He taught them for eight years. Until college.' Sadie turned and took in the room and the lab, the books and the posters that seemed so dated. 'He taught here. And he set up a temporary lab and made inventions, and . . . My dad taught here,' Sadie said one final time, and April wondered what it would be like to be in a place her mother had been – to do the things her mother had done. She had no idea what that must feel like, but she couldn't help but look at Sadie a little differently as she drifted back to her beakers and her clipboard and whatever SadieMatic she was trying to create.

April tried not to feel jealous as she looked down at the shelves again.

These were Gabriel Winterborne's books. His models. His lessons and his childhood – right here, on these shelves and these walls. Like a magnet, her fingers were drawn to the words carved deep into the wood:

Gabriel was here.

Then she found the words below them.

So was Izzy.

'Hello, everyone!' For a second, April thought she must have conjured Ms Nelson, because there she was, sweeping into the room. 'Oh good. You're settling in,' she said when she saw Violet drawing on the blackboard. 'Colin, do you have—'

'A thousand words on the fall of the Roman Empire with an emphasis on the rise of Constantinople? Coming right up.'

'Good,' the woman said, then thought for a moment. 'Oh, Colin? Write it in French.'

April expected Colin to protest, but he just shrugged

and said, '*Oui*,' as if that was the most basic instruction in the world.

Then Smithers came in, a thick stack of papers in his hands. 'Who's ready to take some tests!' He sounded suspiciously like Sadie as he handed papers to Tim and Violet.

April was about to take her seat at the table when Ms Nelson said, 'April? Might I have a word?'

That day the Woman in White was the Woman in Blue, it seemed. Not like the sky outside but like the sea beyond the windows. From her head to her toes she wore the colour, and April felt a sense of calm come over her just by looking at it as she followed Ms Nelson into the hall.

'How are you, April?' Ms Nelson asked. 'Did you recover from the incident at breakfast? Are you burned?'

'Yes. I mean no. I mean yes, I recovered. No, I'm not burned,' she said, because she knew it was the answer Ms Nelson wanted to hear.

'Good. I'm glad. But, April, there's something else I wanted to talk to you about. It's come to my attention that a vase was broken last night.'

Ms Nelson looked at April like she wasn't actually

listening for April's answer – she was watching for April's response, and April was keenly aware of the difference.

'I didn't do it!' she blurted a little too quickly. 'Really. I didn't.'

There was something about the way Ms Nelson was studying her. Not like she was mad. More like she was worried. Not about the vase. But about April. And April didn't like it one bit.

'If you break or spill or stain . . .' Ms Nelson started. 'If you do something like that, you know you can tell me, right? Children live here, April. Things get broken. And torn. And shattered into a million pieces in the middle of the night. Those things happen because life isn't perfect. Kids aren't perfect. I assure you, no adults are. You won't get in trouble for having accidents here. This isn't that kind of home.'

April thought about the long black car and the ragtag group of kids living like kings and queens, the tall gates meant to keep the world at bay. And April couldn't help but think about the question that had been in the back of her mind for twenty-four hours: *Then what kind of home is it?*

But she couldn't ask that, so she just said, 'I didn't break anything.' And Ms Nelson shook her head, as if she couldn't help but be disappointed.

'We don't mind if you have accidents in this house, April. But we mind very much if you *lie*.'

'I didn't do it! It was . . .' *the Sentinel*, April thought but didn't dare say. 'It was already broken. I heard someone, and—'

'So you *were* out of bed last night and wandering the halls?'

'Is being out of bed against the rules?' April shot back.

'No.' Ms Nelson took a ragged breath, then gave April that look again, the one that was filled with pity. 'I hope, in time, that you'll realise you're safe here, April. You don't have to hide things. And you don't have to lie. All I'm asking from you is that you try to believe me. Can you try?'

'Yes, ma'am,' April said, which wouldn't have been so bad, except when she walked back into the classroom, the other kids were acting a little too busy and trying a little too hard to make it seem like they hadn't heard every word Ms Nelson said. Which meant they'd totally heard. Which meant April suddenly felt like turning around and running just as fast and as far as she could.

And she might have done it too – except she felt a tiny hand slipping into hers, holding her there as firmly as if she'd been held by a thousand chains.

'I didn't break the vase,' she said, and Violet smiled, and April knew it was up to her to figure out who did.

HOW TO CATCH AN URBAN LEGEND

April didn't know how to catch the Sentinel, but she knew she wasn't the one who was wandering the halls breaking things, and sometimes a girl's gotta go outside her comfort zone. So Sentinel catching it was.

When sundown came and the house fell asleep under a blanket of darkness and the low, distant howl of the wind, April quietly pushed back the thick velvet curtains that surrounded her bed. She gathered up the handful of things she'd nabbed and grabbed and sneaked throughout the day. Her arms were overflowing and her heart was racing, but she was extra special careful in the hall and on the stairs because the one thing she knew for certain was that you can't catch an urban legend if you're noisy.

At the base of the stairs, she went to work, and then . . . April waited.

Three hours later, her eyes itched and her head felt like it wasn't screwed on straight. She was alone in the little alcove by the door, tucked away behind a container of smelly old umbrellas, shrouded in silence and night. Eventually, her eyes got heavier and heavier, and her head got lower and lower.

I'll just lie down for a little while, April told herself. *It would be a shame to waste this nice hard floor.*

So April did lie down. And April dreamed.

It was a much-better-than-average dream. She was lost in a forest where the tree trunks were sausages and the leaves were a thick, creamy layer of mac and cheese. No one ever yelled at April in that forest. And she knew she'd never have to leave. But then her mother wouldn't find her. And April's mother simply *had* to find her. She would.

She would.

She would.

At first, April wasn't sure why she was screaming. But then she bolted upright and scooted further into the corner. She didn't know why she needed to hide. She just knew she had to save herself because no one else was going to. But save herself from what, she didn't know.

And then she heard the cursing.

And she remembered the Sentinel.

And she realised: fictional vigilantes don't curse.

They certainly don't get caught in booby traps made out of dental floss, Slinkies, fishing nets and old socks. So April wasn't exactly scared as she inched out of her hiding place and towards the figure that was clawing and fighting against the net, mumbling words April didn't really want to understand.

No. At that point, April wasn't scared.

She was *terrified*.

It was like she'd caught a wild animal in her trap and not a man. She might have thought he was a werewolf, except (1) the moon wasn't full, and (2) even a part-man-part-wolf creation would probably look more human than the creature in the net looked then.

His clothes were old and filthy. A thick coarse beard covered his face, and his long hair probably hadn't been combed in years.

Smithers must have missed some of the broken vase from the night before, because when he put his hand on the hard floor and tried to duck beneath the net, he hissed in pain, and when he pulled back, April could see the blood on his palm, all while he continued to twist and kick, even as the dental floss wound tighter and tighter around his ankle. There was no way out, and he must have known it, because he stopped fighting as April inched closer and closer.

And closer.

And that's when she knew that she'd been wrong.

He wasn't a legend. And he wasn't a man. No, April had caught herself a ghost.

'You're Gabriel Winterborne.'

For the first time, he looked straight at her, and April thought about the paintings of the little boy holding his father's hand as if he had no idea that sometimes people let go.

'That's not my name.' The voice was gravelly, like it hadn't been used in a really long time.

'Sure it is,' April said. 'I've seen pictures, you know. From before.' She looked him up and down. 'You got old. And . . . hairy.' He grimaced more at the *old* part than the *hairy* part, and April kept talking. 'But I know who you are. I'm really good with faces.'

Then, in a flash so smooth she could have missed it he pulled a knife from his boot and cut away the net, and then he was up and prowling closer. He had the look of a man with absolutely nothing left to lose – of someone who would leave no witnesses – no survivors – and April scrambled backwards.

Her foot must have gotten tangled in the floss, though. She must have lost her balance. All she really knew for sure was that one minute she was looking at a dead man, and the next she was skidding, sliding, falling through the air until, suddenly, she wasn't.

Hands gripped her shoulders just as a voice called out, saying, 'Hello? Is anyone there?'

There was the sound of soft footsteps on the stairs, and suddenly those hands were picking April up and pressing her against the bottom of the staircase just as the words 'Who's there?' rang out from overhead.

It was Ms Nelson's voice. April recognised it. But she wasn't the only one. They were standing face-to-face, and April looked into eyes full of rage and frustration, hunger and fear.

'Who's there?' This time, Ms Nelson's voice was a warning.

He squeezed his eyes shut, and the hands on her arms went slack. April broke away and stumbled into the light, but the words didn't come.

'It's' – *Gabriel Winterborne!* – 'just me,' she said instead, for reasons she didn't quite know.

Ms Nelson wore white silk pyjamas with a matching robe, but her slippers had been hand-knitted out of rainbow-coloured yarn, and the right one was two sizes bigger than the left.

'April.' She pulled her robe tighter and exhaled like she hadn't even realised she'd been holding her breath. 'You scared me.' She looked around. 'Who were you talking to?'

April couldn't help herself; she glanced at the base of the stairs again – right into Gabriel Winterborne's cool silver gaze.

She watched him shake his head once – twice – slowly. And she thought about how he had broken a vase and gotten her in trouble.

Then she thought about how he might be a very good person to owe her a favour. Finally, she thought about what it must be like to have – and lose – a family and then come home to find out a bunch of kids like April had taken over your house. Plus, she knew exactly how it felt to go to bed hungry. No one – not even werebillionaires – deserved a fate like that.

'No one. Myself. I was talking to myself.'

'Why?' Ms Nelson asked. 'What are you doing up?'

'Oh?' April didn't mean to make her voice crack. She didn't want to cry. Maybe she was just too tired, but when she saw the puddle of empty net and floss and cords, springs and Slinkies and pulleys, it was just too much somehow – like the thin string of hope that had been holding April together for far too long was on the verge of breaking too.

Softly, Ms Nelson descended the stairs and saw the mess that lay on the floor.

'I wanted to make an invention. Like Sadie. Everyone likes Sadie. I wanted everyone to like me too.'

April didn't *try* to burst into tears. She was just that good, she supposed. There couldn't have been any other explanation.

The woman's arms were around her then, pulling her into the soft silk of her shoulder. And when April looked back at the shadows, Gabriel Winterborne was gone. Again.

It wasn't until she was back upstairs and under the covers that she began to wonder if she'd even caught him at all.

A DIFFERENT KIND OF PROBLEM

Five million dollars.

In the classroom the next morning, April sat down with a piece of paper and wrote out all those zeroes, one after the other. She'd never dreamed of having that much money, and she tried to wrap her mind around what it might mean – how much it could buy. But she didn't even know where to begin.

Five thousand. Five million. Five billion. They were all the same to April. And only one fact really mattered: no amount could bring her mother back.

'April.' The word cut through the fog in April's head, but April just kept staring at those zeroes. 'April!' Sadie shouted this time, and April bolted upright. She was on the verge of yelling, *I'm awake*, when Sadie reached for April's paper.

'Smithers said you did very well on your tests, and . . . Ooh, are you doing maths? What kind? Where's the problem?'

The problem was *1 missing billionaire + 1 missing mother + 1 mysterious key ÷ 1 really huge mansion*. April hadn't actually done the maths. She didn't have to, because there, staring her in the face, were five million reasons to stop trying. Except . . .

'April?' Sadie's voice was soft. 'What's wrong?'

'Gabriel Winterborne's worth five million dollars,' April blurted without thinking.

But Sadie simply rolled her eyes. 'Oh, he's worth *way* more than that. Five million is just what Evert's willing to pay to get him back. Gabriel's the sole heir to Winterborne Industries!'

'What about his uncle?'

'Oh, Evert's in charge while Gabriel's missing. But it all belongs to Gabriel. Or that's what Smithers always says whenever Evert comes around.'

April thought about the way Evert had been lovingly caressing a wall when everyone was supposed to be at breakfast. True, April had never had a home before, but she was pretty sure that *wall caressing* wasn't exactly normal, so she asked, 'Does Evert come here a lot?'

'I guess so.' Sadie shrugged. 'He just kind of shows up sometimes and wanders around for a while.'

'Why?'

'I think he's sad. If Gabriel's really dead, then he's the last of the Winterbornes. That's gotta be lonely, you know?'

April did know. And if Sadie was living here, then she probably did too. But April didn't want to think about that, so she focused on how Evert had appeared in the corridor when everyone thought he'd already gone home. How Evert had been skulking around like a ghost. But he definitely wasn't the only one.

'If it's Winterborne House and he's the last surviving Winterborne, why doesn't he live here?'

'Because, technically, Gabriel's *missing*. Not dead. So, legally, things are exactly like they were when Gabriel disappeared. Which means Smithers is in charge of this house and Evert has to live in his own house down the shore. It looks a lot like Winterborne House. But it's smaller. I don't think he likes that random kids get to live in his family's mansion and he's stuck in the mini mansion, but whenever he comes around, he acts like Colin and I aren't even here, so . . .' Sadie gave a shrug like it didn't really matter. And maybe it didn't. But there was something that did, and April didn't quite know how to ask.

'Hey, Sadie . . .' April said gently, 'how long have you been here?'

'Two years.' If Sadie was bothered by the question, it didn't show. 'My parents had a car accident when I was little. I lived with my grandma for a while, but then she got sick, and then, since my parents worked for Winterborne Industries and my dad was Gabriel's tutor and all, Ms Nelson said I should live here.'

'And Colin came a year ago?' April asked. Sadie nodded.

'His mum came, and . . . well . . . he stayed.' Sadie seemed a little sad at that memory, but she brightened when she said, 'And now you're here! And Tim! And Violet! It's so nice . . .' she started, but trailed off, as if maybe she didn't trust April enough to say what came next.

'What's nice?' April prompted.

Sadie looked a little embarrassed but admitted, 'Not being alone.'

April had spent most of her life in group homes, sleeping six girls to a room and waiting thirty minutes for the bathroom. She couldn't imagine being the only kid in a mansion that creaked and moaned and was half dark even in the middle of the day.

She'd never, ever been alone. But she'd always been lonely. So she looked at Sadie and said, 'I'm glad we're here too.'

On the other side of the room, Colin was typing on a laptop and Tim was reading a book. Violet was off somewhere, talking to a doctor that Ms Nelson had brought in just because she thought it might help her feel more at home. April had never been in a house where you got to see a doctor if you weren't bleeding really, really badly.

'Sadie, what would happen if Gabriel Winterborne came back?'

'Well,' Sadie said slowly, as if – for once in her life – she wasn't quite sure about the answer, 'I guess that depends on Gabriel Winterborne.'

THE BUTLER TOTALLY DIDN'T DO IT

'Hello, Smithers.'

'Hello, Miss April. How may I be of service?' He was wearing a white shirt with an apron and black sleeves that went up over the arms of the shirt. Like someone had decided to turn a long-sleeve shirt into a short-sleeve shirt and that was the part that was left over.

But he didn't seem worried that he was wearing leftovers. Nope. He seemed like the happiest guy in the world as he stood on the rolling ladder on the main floor of the library, a feather duster in one hand, humming the kind of song that April highly suspected didn't even have any words.

'Smithers, I was wondering if you might help me.'

'I will do all that I can, miss. What seems to be the problem?'

'I'd like to do some research.'

Smithers practically beamed. 'Excellent. And what, might I ask, are we researching?'

'Gabriel Winterborne.' April didn't mean to blurt it out, but it was too late. The words were ahead of her, and she had to hurry to catch up. 'I mean, I was just wondering . . . Have you worked here for a long time? What was he like? What was his family like? Did he have any hobbies?'

She thought Smithers might tell her to mind her own business, but he just climbed down the ladder and said, 'I had the honour of serving Master Gabriel, yes. And his siblings and parents.' He studied April. 'Is there a reason you are asking?'

'Well . . . yeah . . . I mean . . . I'd like to know more about him. And them. Since I live in their house and all, I'd like to . . . know them.' April tore her gaze away from his. 'If that makes any sense.'

He gave her an approving smile. 'That makes more sense than anything I've heard in quite some time.'

So April sat down at the big wooden table in the centre of the room while Smithers went to work. He gathered scrapbooks and notebooks, old wrinkly newspapers kept in plastic, and photographs pressed into pages.

She saw pictures of babies in hospitals and kids on Christmas morning. She listened to stories about riding bicycles and broken arms. But eventually the pictures stopped. And the stories changed.

TRAGEDY AT SEA
SUMMER STORM DEADLY FOR LOCAL FAMILY
LITTLE BOY FOUND

The oldest newspapers had taken on a yellowish hue that reminded April of how she felt one time after eating tuna salad that had been sitting on the counter way too long. They showed pictures of a smiling, happy family and a big, pretty boat, but they used words like *explosion* and *wreckage*, *search* and *rescue*.

But one word popped up over and over: *survivor*.

April studied the pictures of the little boy who washed up on his family's shore a long time ago, but the man April had met the night before was still a long, long way from home.

And that's how April came to feel sorry for a billionaire.

'It's been twenty years,' Smithers told her. 'But, honestly, it feels like yesterday.'

Then he handed her a different book and started putting

things away while April flipped through page after page of pictures. April watched the little boy change and grow. It was like he got stretched out. His eyes and smile stayed the same, but everything else got bigger.

She watched him morph from a sad little boy to a young man who had a smirking grin and fancy clothes. There were pictures in the society pages with gossip about what girl he was going to take to which gala and how many fancy cars he'd wrecked already that year.

And then the pictures stopped.

And the stories changed.

SOLE SURVIVING WINTERBORNE HEIR MISSING

WINTERBORNE STOCK PLUMMETS AS LEADERSHIP REMAINS UNCERTAIN

LITTLE BOY LOST

The world wanted to know where Gabriel Winterborne went, but as she sat there, newspapers and pictures and magazines spread around her, April asked a different question: *Why did he come back now?*

'Is everything to your satisfaction, Miss April?'

She looked up at Smithers, who had traded his feather duster for a broom.

There was one more newspaper clipping – newer and

fresher than the rest. But Gabriel wasn't in it. Instead, Evert Winterborne stood in the forefront. In the photo, he was wearing a tuxedo. His hair was slicked back, and his arm was around the waist of Ms Nelson.

April scanned the headline: **WINTERBORNE FOUNDATION NAMES NEW HEAD – NEW MISSION.**

But Gabriel Winterborne wasn't mentioned again. As far as the world was concerned, he was just . . . gone.

Only April knew better.

'Do you know where he went, Smithers?'

'No, Miss April, I do not.' He shook his head. 'If Master Gabriel is gone, then it's because he wishes it to be that way, and it is my job to see to the wishes of the Winterborne family. If Master Gabriel is dead . . .' His voice cracked. 'Then I don't want to know.'

'What'll happen if he doesn't come back?'

'Don't you worry about that, April. You have a home now.'

April's home was with her mother. But April had to find her first, and finding her meant finding whatever her key opened. Which meant staying in Winterborne House as long as possible.

'If Gabriel's declared dead, then his uncle will inherit

everything, right? What happens then, Smithers? To the house? To you? To me and Violet and Tim and Sadie and Colin?'

'Ms Nelson is in charge of the Winterborne Foundation now, April. You'll be fine.'

'But we might have to leave Winterborne House?'

Smithers studied her for a long time before he spoke again. 'I assure you, Isabella and I will never put you out on the street. Does it really matter if you live in this house or another?'

April fingered the key that dangled around her neck and didn't say what she was thinking: that, to her, it mattered a whole lot.

YOU CAN CATCH MORE GHOSTS WITH HONEY

Turns out, supposedly dead billionaires who have been missing for ten years are slippery.

After that first night, Gabriel never fell for one of April's traps again. He must have jumped over every threshold and slid through every crack, because he was like a mouse who, night after night, walked away with the cheese without ever getting caught.

It was extremely disappointing.

Because, as far as April could tell, the key to finding her mother was the actual, literal key. And the key had something to do with the Winterbornes. And Gabriel was the only Winterborne she knew besides Evert. And April didn't like Evert, even though she didn't really know why.

April needed Gabriel Winterborne to help her find her mother!

So eventually April gave up on the trap.

And started focusing on the cheese.

When April was six, she'd had a really nice foster mother who'd told her that she'd 'catch more flies with honey', so April started there. She took as many rolls as she could from the breakfast table and a jar of peanut butter from the pantry and a plastic bear full of honey, which seemed appropriate considering how fond Gabriel Winterborne was of growling and all.

She left it all on the table where the vase had been before Gabriel broke it. And then she hid. That night, she tried as hard as she could to stay awake in the tiny alcove with the umbrellas, but when she woke up the next morning, the food was gone and in its place was a note that said *Leave me alone*.

Well, when the honey didn't work, April moved on to cheese, since that was the preferred food for traps it seemed. She left a big wedge of Cheddar on the back stairs with a bunch of bread and a bottle of lemonade, but that disappeared too, even though April swore she never even fell asleep that time.

Every night April tried, and every night April failed, but every time she missed him, she learned something. Sadie had been trying to teach Tim and April about the scientific method, and April told herself she hadn't really messed up – she'd just found half a dozen ways not to catch a billionaire. So she decided to focus on what she'd learned:

1. Gabriel Winterborne was somewhere in the mansion (which was a good thing).
2. The mansion was enormous (which was a bad thing).

It was easy to imagine him living in an attic or under the floorboards or in a closet even Smithers didn't know about. If April could just find out where he was hiding . . . After all, she didn't need to *catch* him. Not exactly. She just needed to *find* him.

Which was when April got her best idea ever.

She wasn't sure what she was expecting when she threw open the door to the big storage closet where Smithers kept the supplies. What she found was shelf after shelf of clean white sheets and fluffy folded towels – so many that April knew one would never be missed. So she started with a pillowcase and a set of the softest sheets that April had ever felt. Next came a bar of soap and some shampoo that smelled like vanilla, a nail file, a comb, and a ponytail holder, because April always felt way better when she could keep her hair out of her eyes.

She also threw in four hard-boiled eggs, three chicken legs (though where Smithers had found a three-legged chicken April had no idea), two apples, and a bottle of water that had bubbles in it and made you burp but in the good way.

And salt. April never, ever ate hard-boiled eggs without salt.

Or so she told herself.

She left the pillowcase, stuffed completely full and smelling like barbecued cake, in a place she knew he would see it. And then she went upstairs and climbed into her real bed, safe and sound. When she woke a few hours later, she ran downstairs and found the pillowcase gone. But, this time, April smiled.

Because even though Smithers probably wouldn't have approved of April punching a hole in the bottom of that pillowcase and no one likes the idea of wasting perfectly good salt, when April dropped to the floor, she could see the thin white trail running across the dark floor of the mansion, streaming along, showing the way.

And April being April, she followed.

Through the foyer and past the library and down the twisty stairs that led to the narrow hall that, Sadie said, was the oldest part of the mansion.

The salt line was faint but very much there – right up until the point when it wasn't.

It disappeared into thin air. Except. Not thin air. Into a fireplace that didn't have a fire, and April had to wonder if Gabriel Winterborne might be a little bit like Santa.

All around April, Winterborne House was still sleeping. In just a few hours, Smithers would be up and cooking breakfast. Sadie, Colin, Violet, and Tim would be coming downstairs to eat. But right then the only things that moved were the hands of the big grandfather clock and the dust that danced in the light of the moon, hoping Smithers might miss it.

April looked back down at the salt line, and she thought about Gabriel Winterborne. Not the man. The boy. Winterborne House was lonely. Too dark and too formal, too close to the cliffs and the sea. On edge in almost every sense of the word, and April felt sad. Not just for herself.

But for the little boy who must have lived here when Winterborne House was an orphanage for one. That boy would have explored. That boy would have run wild. That boy would have found every nook and cranny, crease and crevice, and that boy was still hiding from the outside world.

The difference was that, this time, someone was going to come looking.

She took a step closer to the fireplace and studied it again – not the whole, but the pieces. She pushed against the angel's wing and pulled on the candlesticks that sat atop the mantel. She pressed every stone and touched every square, until, finally, April stepped back and sighed and admitted to herself that she'd been wrong.

Then she noticed the salt was moving, drifting across the floor like the house was trying to blow out its birthday candles. But houses don't breathe. They do, however, have draughts.

As she eased back towards the fireplace, she noticed a book on the shelves beside it. **HIDDEN PASSAGEWAYS OF MEDIEVAL ENGLAND** the spine said, and April pulled on the book, thinking, *Could it really be that easy?*

(Spoiler alert: it wasn't.)

The fireplace stayed closed, and April groaned in frustration, kicking the cast-iron poker that was there for a log that didn't burn. A poker that didn't fall but rather, *tilted* with a pop as the fireplace swung open, revealing a very dark, very windy, very dusty, very scary passageway.

It was the most beautiful thing that April had ever seen, and she stepped into the darkness, smiling all the way.

BECAUSE *BILLIONAIRE* RHYMES WITH *LAIR*

It wasn't a hallway, and it wasn't a corridor. It certainly didn't feel like the rest of the house. It was more like a cave or a tunnel that sloped down into the earth. The floor was cold and hard against her feet, and she kept one hand on the damp stone wall as she inched towards a light that flickered in the distance.

With every step, the air got colder and damper, and a part of April was afraid that a wave might wash up and carry her out to sea. But she kept walking anyway.

Water dripped from the ceiling, a steady *plop*, *plop*, *plop* that echoed, and April wished she'd brought Mr Winterborne some soup. It was the kind of place where you could only hope to be warm on the inside.

When the tunnel opened into a big cavernous space,

April stopped. A fire burned in a stone fireplace on the far side of the room, and she watched the flickering light dance over the tall, arching ceiling. More tunnels branched off, stretching out to who knew where, and April turned slowly, taking everything in.

Until she heard the words that stopped her. 'You're not as stupid as you look.'

The light was so dim that it took her a second to find him in the shadows, sitting on an overturned crate, the pillowcase beside him. The voice sounded like Winterborne House looked: smooth and elegant, rich and cultured. It sounded like the voice of a movie star. But the body it came from looked like something that had been carried in by the sea and tossed up on the rocks below. Battered. Bruised. And just barely hanging together as he leaned into the light.

'Uh . . . thank you?' April said when she couldn't think of anything else. He was gnawing on a chicken leg, and when he was finished, he tossed the bone on to the fire, sending sparks up like fireflies. Then he dug back into the bag, pulled out a piece of bread, and bit into it like it might be the last thing he'd ever eat.

'Don't thank me,' he said with his mouth full. 'A dog is

smarter than I thought you were.'

When he bit another hunk out of the bread and chased it with another chicken leg, April wanted to tell him that it would take one to know one, but she didn't want to tempt her luck. He might decide to bite *her* next if she wasn't careful, so instead she asked, 'What is this place?'

He held his hands out wide. 'It's Winterborne House, the illustrious home of my illustrious family. Don't you recognise a mansion when you see one?'

Maybe it was the look in his eyes or his long greasy hair and ragged beard, the black coat that was fraying at the edges, or the fingerless gloves that held the precious food, but for the first time April wondered if maybe Smithers and Ms Nelson had locked him down here because it was better for the world to think him dead than to know for a fact that he was crazy.

But when he saw the look on her face, he laughed. And it was the most sane sound she'd ever heard him make.

'We're in the cellars, April. They run all under the house. They've been blocked off for decades.'

Then the wind blew again, too hard to call it a draught, and April shivered.

'For good reason,' he said, digging into the pillowcase

again and pulling out an apple.

April looked at the madman who sounded like a professor or a politician or . . . a billionaire.

'Why are you here?'

Apple juice ran down his chin, and she thought he might choke on the apple's core, but he just brought the tattered sleeve of his filthy coat up and wiped his face.

'The same reason you're here. There's a price on my head. Oh, don't pretend you didn't know. Thanks to dear Uncle Evert, the whole world knows. But if you've come to collect your thirty pieces of silver, you should know' – he made a show of patting his pockets – 'I must have left my chequebook in my other coat.'

April rolled her eyes. 'I mean, why are you *here*? This is your house, right? *You're a billionaire!* Don't you have a bedroom with silk sheets and . . . you know . . . a shower upstairs?'

For a long time he was too silent. Too still. 'I'm not here, April. I'm nowhere.'

'Everyone thinks you're dead.'

But then the strangest thing happened: he smiled. His eyes twinkled, and he was handsome, almost charming, as he said, 'I know.'

131

April didn't mean to step closer. Her body just did that sometimes, move without her permission. Because even filthy and smelly as he was, Gabriel Winterborne was like a magnet, drawing trouble to him, and April had been told by at least six different foster mothers that Trouble was her middle name.

'But you're *not* dead.' It seemed like a fairly important point, but he just shook his head.

'The Winterbornes died, April. Everybody knows that.' He couldn't face her when he said it, April noticed. He acted busy, rummaging in the pillowcase, pulling out the soap and the razor, the cheese and the scissors. And when he said, 'Thank you for the food,' it was almost like it was hard to admit that she'd actually helped. That the big bad billionaire had needed the little girl who wore her entire net worth around her neck.

'Though I must admit' – he levelled her with a glare – 'I would have preferred it if you'd forgotten the *salt*.'

She might have blushed if she hadn't been so desperate.

'I can get you more food,' she told him. 'And clothes. And anything else you need.'

'I don't need anything. Now go back to bed. It's late – or early. Smithers will start looking for you eventually,

and, trust me, you don't want Smithers looking for you.'
For a split second she saw him as the little boy he must have
been once. 'And don't come back here. Ever again.'

'Ms Nelson is suspicious!' April blurted. 'She knows
someone's been sneaking around. She's smart, you know.'

A sad smile crossed his face. 'Oh, I know.'

It hurt him to hear the woman's name, so she didn't say
it again. She just warned, 'Someone will catch you if you
keep sneaking around.'

'So?' He was rising to his feet. 'As you've said, it is
my house.'

'But you're dead,' she reminded him, and the scary
glare morphed into a mischievous gleam.

'I am indeed.'

'So you need me. To get you food and stuff. Even dead
men have to eat, it looks like.'

'And why would you help me?' he snapped. 'Money?
Evert will give you five million, but maybe you think I'll
give you six to hold your tongue?'

'I don't want your money!'

His laugh was colder than the wind. 'Everyone wants
my money.'

'I need your help!'

It was the honest truth, but he looked at her like she was playing a joke on him – a mean one.

'I can't help you, April. I can't help anyone.'

'No. You can help me,' she said. Before she even realised what she was doing, she was reaching for her key, but the chain was tangled in her hair, so April jerked. She felt the chain break, but she didn't care. She just held up her key and pleaded, 'I have this! And I need you to help me find out what it opens.'

For a moment, he stood perfectly still, staring at April and the small key in her hand as if both of them were figments of his imagination. His mouth was agape, and his breath came harder, and it felt like, in that moment, the room went from cold to hot.

April was definitely getting warmer.

'My mum left this for me. That's the Winterborne crest, right?' She pointed at the part of the key that had matched the tiny box at the museum. 'So it came from here, didn't it? I bet she was a maid or something. I bet she left me something here – in this house – and I need you to help me find it.'

For a second, April felt strong and sure. But then Gabriel Winterborne laughed at her.

'Have you *seen* Winterborne House? Really seen it? Because I grew up here. This was my playground and schoolroom and home, and there are rooms I've never set foot in.'

'But this key opens something, and with your help—'

'Go to bed, April. Just . . . forget I'm here. Forget I even exist. The world almost has, and the sooner the job is done, the better.'

He actually sounded like he meant it. Like he believed it. But April didn't have time to feel sorry for anyone. April had a full-time job just taking care of herself. And if he wanted to sleep on the floor and eat scraps and not wash his hair, then that was his business.

Finding her mother was April's.

'You're going to help me find my mother,' April said as if she, the twelve-year-old orphan, had the power to make the grown-up billionaire do exactly what she wanted him to do. 'You're going to help me, or I'm going to tell the world that Gabriel Winterborne is alive and well and . . . smells.'

She watched him listen to her words and register her threat. She even saw him recoil a little bit at the smelly part. He was one of the richest men in the world, but in that moment, he was a man who had absolutely nothing left to lose.

It was a look April totally knew when she saw it.

She wanted to argue. She wanted to plead. She was even willing to beg, but he was too fast and too strong, and the next thing she knew, he was swooping down and picking her up, tossing her over his shoulder like she weighed no more than that pillowcase.

'I'll do it!' She banged against his back and yelled louder. 'I'll put it on the internet! I'll call the newspapers! I'll take pictures and videos and tell everyone you're crazy and living in the basement—'

'Cellars.'

She stopped banging. 'I won't even do it for the money. I'll tell the world that you're down here just because you're mean.'

'I believe you, April.' He sounded almost impressed.

'I'll do it!' she shouted into the void. 'I'll tell. I'll—'

But before April could finish, the fireplace was opening again and she was being dropped unceremoniously on to the floor. The cellar seemed a million miles away, even though the cold wind still blew through the open passage.

'There's a storm coming. Now go to bed and forget

you know me. Forget you saw me. Forget I'm alive.'
He looked back into the darkness. 'Forget I was ever
alive at all.'

17

A KNIFE AS SHARP AS LIGHTNING

April did go to bed. Not because he'd told her to but because she was sleepy and the storm had started to blow hard outside the window.

She hoped he was miserable. Cold and wet. Maybe the waves would crash up high enough to flood the cellars and take Gabriel Winterborne far away again.

April told herself that would suit her just fine. She didn't need him anyway. So she pulled the velvet curtains tight around her bed and tucked the covers in around herself and closed her eyes.

She should have slept. She was exhausted, after all. She'd been trying so hard to trap Gabriel Winterborne that her bed should have felt like the best thing ever. But April didn't sleep. Instead, she tossed. She turned. She counted sheep and got up to go to the bathroom. It wasn't until she was on her way back that she noticed that her bed wasn't the only one that was empty.

'Hey, Violet,' she said, inching towards the little girl who was standing at the windows.

Lightning crashed outside, sending bright white light through the glass and over Violet's face. Her eyes looked even bigger as she stared out at the storm.

'Can't you sleep?' April asked, and Violet shook her head. 'Want me to go get Tim?' April asked, but Violet's warm hand was slipping into April's.

'I hate storms.'

They were the first words she'd ever spoken just to April, and for a moment, April stood there, unsure what to say.

Then the words 'Me too,' came from behind them.

Sadie rubbed her eyes and stumbled out of bed. She wore red pyjamas with $E = MC^2$ all over them and was wrapping a blanket around her shoulders as she walked towards the windows.

The rain was coming harder then, falling against the glass like waves, and April could feel Violet's hand start to shake.

'Winterborne House is really old, right, Sadie?'

At first, Sadie looked confused, but April shot her eyes down at Violet and Sadie seemed to take the hint.

'Oh, yeah. It's been here for for ever.'

'It's probably stood through lots of storms, right?'

'Totally,' Sadie went on. 'Hurricanes and thunderstorms and earthquakes. Winterborne House isn't going anywhere, and neither are we.' She dropped to the floor – her eyes at Violet's level before looking up. 'Right, April?'

But April *was* going someplace. Just as soon as she found her mother.

So she stayed quiet as Sadie and Violet piled pillows on the floor. She wordlessly helped drag blankets off of beds and arranged them in front of the big bay windows. No one seemed to notice April's silence as they nestled together, lulled to sleep by the sounds of the storm.

In hindsight, April wasn't sure which came first, the rain or the screaming.

One moment, she was sound asleep, and the next, she was bolting awake, tangled in a knot of limbs and pyjamas while the wind crashed through the windows and rain streaked across the room, drenching the floor where they lay. April's hair whipped around her face, clinging to her skin and blinding her. It was like they were in the middle of the storm and not their bedroom, but Violet was up on her knees, shaking and shouting, 'Tiiiimmmmmm!'

'Shh, Violet. It's—'

But that was when April saw the knife.

The room was dark except for the flashes of lightning that came through the windows – bursting with the boom of the thunder, reflecting off of a silver blade that floated through the darkness. The curtains around April's bed billowed in the wind, and the knife slashed at them, cutting away the ropes of Sadie's invention, sending them crashing to the floor.

And, through it all, Violet kept screaming. 'No!'

'What's happening?' Sadie pushed upright and sleepily reached for the glasses she wore when she didn't want to mess with her contacts. But the wind and the rain were too hard and the glasses slipped from her hand. 'Darn it,' Sadie exclaimed as she dropped back to the floor, feeling her way through the soggy blankets.

But April . . . April kept her eyes on the blade.

And the blade was taking a step closer to her.

There was shouting in the hallway. Doors banged open.

141

Then a massive bolt of lightning struck – a blinding white light that came at the same time as the thunder – and the whole house seemed to shake. The hallway lights flickered on then off just as the door to their room burst open.

'Violet!' Tim shouted.

'What's going on?' Colin asked, but the room was so dark April couldn't even see him.

She could only feel the rush of air as someone ran past her in the darkness. She could only hear the crunch of the glass beneath feet and see a dark figure rushing for the broken window.

And then the flash of the knife was gone.

'What happened?' Ms Nelson stood in the doorway, a candelabra in each hand – one burning bright with candles and the other dangling by her side like a sword. 'Girls, what—'

April looked at the broken window, the scattered glass, and rain-soaked pillows and blankets. Then she looked at Violet, who muttered, 'He was here.'

'Who?' Tim asked.

'The Sentinel,' Violet said, and everyone exhaled.

'Smithers, the generator?' Ms Nelson called down the hallway.

April heard him call back, 'It might take a few minutes to—'

But before he'd even finished, there was a clicking sound and the lights in the hallway flickered to life. Ms Nelson reached for the switch, and light filled the disaster area formerly known as their bedroom.

Smithers swept in then. Literally. He had a broom and dustpan and started cleaning away the broken glass.

'Another window gone,' he said to no one in particular.

'The Sentinel broke it,' Violet said as Tim picked her up and carried her away from the broken glass, placing her on her bed.

Ms Nelson knelt down in front of her. 'No, sweetheart. It's OK. These old windows just break sometimes if the temperature drops too quickly and the rain and wind are—'

'My bed!' Sadie cried as she rushed to where her velvet hangings were strewn across the floor. One of the ropes had run through the pulleys and got wrapped around the ceiling fan that was spinning in the wind. April's own bed was a mess of blankets and pillows and bed curtains, everything twisted and broken and torn.

'I'm sorry, Sadie,' Ms Nelson said. 'The wind must have—'

'It wasn't the wind,' Violet said, stronger now. 'It was the Sentinel.'

'No, sweetheart.' Ms Nelson ran a hand through Violet's damp hair. 'I know that must have been awfully scary, but the wind just pulled the curtains and they got tangled in the ropes and it caused a chain reaction. It wasn't the Sentinel, sweetheart. I promise. The Sentinel isn't real.'

But Violet just looked up at April, as if it was going to have to be their little secret.

Eventually, Smithers covered the window with plywood and the girls moved to another room – all three of them piled into the biggest bed that April had ever seen, but April lay in the darkness until the storm was just a rumble in the distance.

Ms Nelson was right: the Sentinel wasn't real. But there was another knife-wielding madman of April's acquaintance.

And he had a lot of explaining to do.

THE WEIGHT OF WHAT'S NOT THERE

It was too hot. At first, April thought she was back in the fire, flames bearing down on her from all directions. But the air was clean, and her eyes didn't burn. And she was pretty sure someone was trying to shove an elbow up her nose. And someone else was shoving a knee through her back. But it was the thing April didn't feel that scared her.

She bolted upright in bed and looked down at her clenched fist – at the place where her key was supposed to be. And she remembered the broken chain and the storm – the broken window, the man. And the knife.

'Where's your key?' Violet pointed to April's neck, and April knew why her fist was empty.

'No,' she said, throwing off the covers and running

down the hall.

Plywood covered the window and the broken glass was gone, but the bedroom still looked like it had been in a storm. Covers were askew. Bed curtains hung at odd angles, and everything was soggy. Pieces of Sadie's inventions were scattered all over the room, blown by the wind and the rain. But none of that mattered to April.

She ran to her own bed and ransacked the sheets and blankets. She tossed aside the pillows. She looked under the bed and on the dresser, beneath the pile of dirty clothes that hadn't made it into the hamper and inside her emergency jar of peanut butter that even Smithers didn't know about.

April looked everywhere.

But April already knew.

Her key was missing. No. Not *missing*. Because, in her heart, April knew exactly where it was.

She remembered taking it off in the cellar. She remembered showing it to Gabriel Winterborne. She remembered the broken chain and how she'd set it aside to fix in the morning. And then she remembered the storm. And the knife.

'April?' Sadie said from the doorway, Violet beside her. 'What's wrong?'

'Nothing's wrong.' (*Something was wrong.*) 'I'm fine.' (*She wasn't fine.*)

'I think something is wrong,' Sadie said, because Sadie was a scientist, descended from a long line of scientists. Observation was in her blood.

'No. It's . . . I just lost—'

'Your key's gone!'

April hadn't even realised that Sadie knew about her key. She tried to keep it tucked away, hidden. Because in April's experience, the only way to keep something safe was to keep it secret. But Sadie had noticed. Because Sadie wasn't just a scientist. She was also a friend.

But April had never really had one of those before, so she blurted, 'It's no big deal.' (*It was a big deal.*)

'We'll help you look for it,' Sadie offered. 'I've been meaning to experiment with—'

'No!' April didn't mean to snap. She certainly didn't mean to make Sadie's eyes get all big and weepy. 'Really, Sadie. It's OK. I'll find it,' April said, because in that moment, it was the one thing she was sure of. 'I know exactly where to look.'

It wasn't until Sadie was halfway down the hall that Violet asked, 'The Sentinel took it, didn't he?'

'Yes,' April said.

'Are you afraid of him?'

'No.' April took Violet's hand. 'He needs to be afraid of me.'

April had a secret. And a problem. She'd thought and worried and wondered most of the day until, finally, she sat perfectly still while Colin stood on top of a chair at the kitchen table, one of Smithers's black coats around his shoulders like a cape.

'And then the Sentinel swooped down . . .' He jumped off the chair and ran around the room. 'Like a . . . *thing that swoops*. Breaking through the window like the storm. Sword drawn!'

A long French baguette came out from underneath Colin's coat/cape, and he brandished it with a flourish.

'And he crept through the room like a . . . *thing that creeps*. Searching for vengeance and . . . *little girls!*' he whispered to Violet.

Tim tensed and Sadie held her breath, but Violet actually laughed. Maybe because the sun was still out and the kitchen was warm and they'd been listening to Colin's tale of adventure all day long, hearing it get more and more absurd with every telling, and now no one knew where the truth stopped and Colin's story began.

No one, that was, except April.

April knew way, way, way too much.

She'd seen the man. And the knife. And the look in Gabriel Winterborne's eyes when she'd shown him her mother's key. Then a few hours later, he'd snuck into her room, and now the key was gone? April didn't believe in coincidence. Bad luck? Yes. That she knew like the back of her hand. But coincidence? Never.

So April was very quiet and very still as she sat there trying to decide what to do.

Part of her wanted to call up Uncle Evert and claim her five million dollars.

Part of her wanted to cry because her key was gone and the only person she'd ever asked for help had taken it.

And part of her just wanted to storm the cellar and take back what was hers from that knife-wielding madman, but . . .

Knife. Wielding. Madman.

So April didn't do anything except sit. And think. And try to figure out what Gabriel Winterborne was up to.

After all, he could have killed them last night

while they slept.

But he didn't.

He could have struck her down in that dirty, empty cellar and tossed her body over the cliffs before anyone even realised she was missing.

But he hadn't.

He could have let her burn to a crisp that night in the museum and taken her key for himself, but instead he'd put it back around her neck and carried her to safety.

And April couldn't stop asking one question: *Why?*

'April, what's wrong?' Ms Nelson was looking at April's plate that was still mostly full of a dish Colin called Smithers Surprise but was really just pasta with meat and cheese and sauce all baked together until it was gooey and delicious. There had been a time when April might have dreamed of such a thing, but now . . .

'I'm not hungry.'

Every single one of them stopped eating.

'I'll call Dr Andrews.' Smithers pushed away from the table.

'No!' April looked around. 'I'm OK.' But April wasn't OK, and more than anything she was terrified that everyone would see it. 'I'm just . . . tired. I didn't sleep so well.'

'It's because of the Sentinel,' Violet said.

'Sweetheart.' Ms Nelson leaned close to Violet. 'I know last night was scary, but the Sentinel isn't real. It wasn't him.'

'But—'

'It was Gabriel Winterborne.'

And just like that, they all turned and looked at April like she was crazy. And April knew what she had to do.

'He's back,' she said, decision made. 'And he's been sneaking around at night, and—'

'April—' Ms Nelson started in a tone that April knew too well.

'It's true! He's the one who broke the vase. He was in our room last night, and—'

'April, I told you, the wind—'

'It was Gabriel Winterborne! I'm not joking! Here. I'll show you!'

By that point, April wasn't actually thinking. It was like her feet had a mind of their own and April was along for the ride as she led the procession from the kitchen and through the halls to the room with the stone fireplace.

'You'll see. He's down here,' she said, taking hold of

the fireplace poker and pulling and . . . falling right on her hind end, the poker still in her hand. For a second she just lay there, staring at it. 'No. That's not right.' She got up and went to the fireplace again, tried to put the poker back in the holder, but that didn't work. Then she started kicking the stone.

'It opens,' she said. 'I swear. It's a secret passageway.'

'Uh, April . . .' Sadie started slowly.

'It's a secret passageway! I'm not making it up!' She could feel the draught coming through the gaps in the stones. She could see the ashes blowing across the floor. 'Look! Feel the wind? See that dust moving? That's because this fireplace opens and Gabriel Winterborne is down there!' She pulled and twisted and pried, but the fireplace didn't budge.

'Sweetheart.' Ms Nelson leaned down and grabbed April's hands, stopping her frantic movements and forcing April to look into her eyes. 'I know it would be worth a lot of money to find him, but—'

'I'm not doing it for the money! I'm doing it because . . .' Everyone was staring at her. Some looked at April like she was crazy, and some looked at her like she was pitiful, but absolutely no one looked at her like she was telling the truth.

'Miss April is absolutely right,' Smithers said at last, and April couldn't help herself.

She cried, 'I am?'

'Indeed. There is a secret passageway behind this fireplace. You were very smart to find it.'

'See! He's—'

'But it's been closed up for decades, April,' Smithers went on, cutting her off. 'It's not safe, and no one is down there. Certainly not Gabriel Winterborne.'

'But he's back,' April said again. 'I've seen him! I talked to him! I—'

'Stop!' Ms Nelson wasn't smiling any more. Her eyes weren't kind, and her words weren't soft as she warned, 'I told you, April. We can tolerate a lot in this house, but not lying.' She swallowed hard. Her voice cracked. 'Especially about him.'

Then Ms Nelson walked away – from the passageway and April and the secret she'd been carrying for days just to have it tossed back in her face like a piece of useless garbage.

'April?' Sadie's voice was just a whisper. 'I've been planning a surprise. You can help me with it if you want to?'

'No thanks, Sadie.'

'Really. It's not a SadieMatic – I promise.' Sadie laughed a little. 'It'll be fun. Please. I . . .'

Sadie looked at Colin for help, but he just said, 'She didn't mean it.' April didn't have to ask him who he meant. 'Everybody's got a thing, you know? Something that hurts real bad if you press on it. He's hers. That's all. She wasn't mad you were wrong. She was mad at herself for wishing you were right.'

Tim and Violet were already out the door. Smithers was gone, doing whatever it was that Smithers did. Then Colin and Sadie walked away, their footsteps echoing down the hallway, until it was just April and the stones and the wind whistling through the gaps, and she couldn't hold her anger back any longer.

'I know what you did!' she shouted.

Maybe she really was going crazy because she had the distinct impression that the stones laughed back. So April pushed against them, yelling louder. 'You didn't have to steal it! I would have given it to you. I would have trusted you! I would have—'

But then April couldn't yell any more because the fireplace was moving and April was falling through the air, tumbling into the darkness.

And on to the floor.

At the feet of a man that maybe she didn't want to find after all.

WHAT YOU DON'T WANT IN A
KNIFE-WIELDING MADMAN

'Oh, April. What am I going to do with you?'

Gabriel Winterborne sounded the same, but he looked different. His hair was still long and his clothes were still ragged, but his eyes were clearer and he moved with purpose, which, April realised, wasn't what you wanted in a knife-wielding madman.

She scrambled back but heard the scrape of the fireplace slamming closed behind her. There was nothing but the cold draught and the dripping water and the man she'd last seen with a knife at four a.m.

But the weird thing was that April still didn't have the good sense to be afraid. Nope. She was way too busy being angry.

'You didn't have to steal it.'

He cocked an eyebrow and actually grinned. 'Steal what?'

'I came to you for help, and you broke into our room! You scared Violet! She's just a little girl.'

'Oh, *she's* a little girl?'

'Don't try to deny it,' she snapped. 'I saw you. I saw *the knife.*'

And just like that, his expression changed, like it had never occurred to him that he might actually get caught.

So April added for good measure, 'I know you took my key. Don't tell me it was the wind or whatever. The wind didn't break that window—'

'It's an old house, April. Old houses are draughty,' he said, but he couldn't look her in the eye.

'I suppose the bed hangings ripped themselves?'

He glared. 'Is that why you decided to turn on me?'

'I didn't turn on you! You broke into my room and stole my key and . . . I know what goes bump in the night.' She looked him up and down. 'And I know where he lives.'

He slumped against the wall and whispered, 'So do I, April. So do I.'

April had seen him dirty and hungry and tired and

bleeding, but she'd never seen him look like that – like he'd just skipped to the last chapter and found out he wasn't ever going to get a happy ending. She might have even felt sorry for him, except . . .

'I want my key,' she said again, because he might have been a knife-wielding madman, but without that key, April wasn't anything at all.

But he just shook his head. 'Get out.'

'I'm not leaving without my mother's key! I'm—'

'You're going to leave.' He pushed away from the wall.

'You're going to walk away, and I'm going to board up this entrance, and you will never come back here again. You will never bring . . . *her* . . . back here, do you hear me? As far as Isabella Nelson is concerned, I'm a dead man. And I'm going to stay that way if it kills me.'

Then she was upside down again, slung over his shoulder as the fireplace slid open. A split second later, she was falling back on to the floor, as if the last fourteen hours hadn't happened at all.

But they *had* happened.

April reached for her key, but it was still missing, and the stones weren't laughing any more.

★ ★ ★

Smithers must not have been doing a very good job of dusting, because her throat burned and her eyes watered. April wanted to wipe the tears away, even though she absolutely was not crying. She was just walking and thinking and making a plan, because she'd wasted enough time already.

She'd get her key back. She had to. But in the meantime, she'd start looking for the lock. She'd start right then – that very moment. She'd start on the first floor and work her way up. Room by room. Wall by wall. Shelf by shelf.

April had made it twelve years without any help from anyone, and the thing that made her maddest was that she'd let herself forget it. Well, she wasn't going to forget it ever again.

So April got to work.

She looked in stuffy rooms with cold fireplaces and the kind of furniture you should never put your feet on. And she searched in bathrooms with soft towels and soap that smelled like flowers. She spent twenty minutes poking an old piano and five trying to open a cabinet that held nothing but dusty board games and about a dozen decks of cards.

April searched and scoured and hunted until she reached a wide corridor that ran along the back of the house, and then April had to stop. And look. And think. Because parts of the wall were lighter than other parts, and something just seemed . . . *off* about the space.

'Don't mind that,' came a voice from behind her, and April turned to find Colin there, studying her as she studied the wall.

'What?' April asked.

'Those spots on the wall. You're not imagining them. That's where the paintings were.'

'What paintings?' April asked, even though she was pretty sure she already knew the answer.

'The ones that burned up in the museum. You heard about the museum, didn't you?'

'Yeah,' April muttered. 'I heard about that.'

Suddenly, April's skin felt too hot – like she was back in the fire. Because Colin wasn't just looking at her – he was seeing her, and April didn't like it one bit. And when he asked, 'You OK, April?' she honestly didn't know what to say, because he'd known when the Fake Fiancée was lying, but he hadn't known when April was telling the truth.

Or maybe he just hadn't cared.

'I'm—'

'There you are!' Sadie's voice came echoing down the hallway. 'Where were you? We looked everywhere!'

'Just wandering around,' April blurted, sounding a little too defensive.

'Well, now that we've found you, we can start!'

'Start what?'

'Movie night!' Sadie looped her arm with April's and started down the hall. 'That's my big surprise. Gabriel Winterborne had a room turned into a cinema!'

'He did?' April asked, because that didn't sound like the man she knew at all. But she didn't actually know Gabriel Winterborne, did she? And that was just part of the problem.

'The bad news is that the movies are really old, but that's OK. A lot of them are classics now. Smithers let me make popcorn! And there's candy and . . .' Sadie trailed off, and when she spoke again, the words were almost a whisper. 'Are you OK? You aren't embarrassed, are you? About . . . before?'

Well, April hadn't been, but she was now, and that made her feel even worse than usual.

'It's like Colin said. Gabriel's just kind of a sore spot. Everything's going to be OK, though. You'll see. We'll watch some movies and eat some popcorn, and it'll be fun.'

And it probably would have been, except, at that moment, April saw something out the windows.

The mansion sat in a cove, rocky cliffs forming a kind of horseshoe on either side with the cold grey water stretching out to the horizon. The sun was getting low, so at first she thought her eyes might have been playing tricks on her. But, no. A door was swinging open. Except it wasn't a door at all. It was more like a section of stones that moved. Just like the fireplace. And then someone emerged, hunching low and running fast, skirting over the edge of the cliffs.

'April?' Sadie's voice was louder.

'Sorry,' April said. 'I've got to . . . I'm not feeling very well. I think I'll go to bed.' She started down the hall, but something made her stop, turn back. 'Have fun with the movie.'

And then she was gone.

THE MINI MANSION

April ran to the closet by the front door and grabbed a dark coat and a black beret, pulled them on, then darted outside before Smithers or Ms Nelson could catch her, before Colin or Tim or Sadie could tell her that she was being stupid. But April wasn't stupid. April was desperate.

If Gabriel Winterborne was taking her key somewhere, then April had to know, and there wasn't a moment to lose.

The sun was dipping low on the horizon, and soon the sky would be totally dark, but that was Future April's problem, she decided. Present April had more important things to worry about.

As it was, Gabriel had a head start. And he was . . . you

know . . . a grown man with way longer legs. Plus, he'd been raised on that rocky shore. So Gabriel had an advantage, no doubt about it. But April had never let being at a disadvantage stop her, and she wasn't about to start now.

She stayed low as she skirted along the cliffs. Every now and then, she could hear a skittering rock or flapping bird, something to tell her that she wasn't alone, even though the mansion was lost on the other side of the twisting ridge and the sound of Sadie's voice was just a memory. April wasn't enjoying movie night. April felt like she was *in* movie night, and she wasn't going back. Not until she had some answers.

She'd find out where he went. She'd see if he used her key. And then she'd go get Ms Nelson and Smithers and all of the kids. She'd show them that Gabriel Winterborne really was alive, and no one would call her a liar ever again.

When she crested the next ridge, she saw it. Lights growing brighter as the sky grew darker, and April's first thought was to stop and look behind her, to wonder how she could have gotten so totally turned around because she'd just *left* Winterborne House. How in the world had she walked down the coast for twenty minutes, only to end up right back *at* Winterborne House?

It didn't make any sense! But then she remembered what Sadie had said – that Uncle Evert lived down the shore in a house that looked a lot like Winterborne House, only smaller.

So April lay on the ground at the top of the ridge and studied the mini mansion. It looked almost like a doll's house perched at the edge of the world. The fog was a ghostly white veil that was floating on the wind, and April knew she wasn't supposed to be there. But she also knew it would be impossible for her to be anywhere else – not when Mr Winterborne might be in the mini mansion right that moment using her mother's key and taking away April's birthright.

So April didn't turn around and go back. Nope. April crept closer.

The wind was cold, and she pulled her coat tighter and her beret lower. She needed to be warm, sure, but she needed to be invisible even more.

She wasn't really thinking as she ran, clinging to the bushes and the rocky ledge until she reached the side of the house. The other kids were probably eating popcorn with all the butter they wanted. They were no doubt drinking the bubbly lemonade and watching movies about singing squirrels or whatever. April didn't much care for singing squirrels, but she loved butter and lemonade, and she hated being cold and . . . worrying. April was so very worried. But that didn't stop her from creeping closer.

She heard a door open. A light flicked on. And then Evert Winterborne was stepping out on to a wide stone patio, checking the pocket watch that he wore on a chain and looking out over the water at the fog that was rolling in like a wave. He seemed impatient. And nervous. And he should have been. Because he definitely wasn't alone.

April might have thought it was a gargoyle perched on the eaves of the house, but gargoyles don't have coats that billow in the wind. They don't fidget. And they're almost never holding swords.

Moonlight glistened off the blade, and April's heart went from pounding to not beating at all. She couldn't breathe. Maybe because she didn't want to risk someone seeing the way her breath turned white in the chilly air. Or maybe she'd just forgotten how. All she really knew for certain was that Gabriel Winterborne had his uncle in his sights, and April didn't know what to do.

On the patio, Evert checked his watch again. Gabriel looked ready to pounce. And April heard footsteps.

Someone was walking around the side of the house. Coming closer and closer. April looked from where Gabriel crouched on the roof to where Evert waited, both unaware of the person approaching in the darkness.

Gabriel shifted. April saw him start to jump. And for some reason, her fingers reached for a small stone and threw it before she could think about what she was doing.

The stone pinged off the terrace, and Evert spun, searching the night. 'Who's there?' he called.

And the night called back, 'It's just me, Evert.'

April crouched down behind a big rock as Ms Nelson walked across the long dark lawn and into the circle of light. Overhead, Gabriel stilled, and Evert called, 'Izzy! To what do I owe the honour?'

He glanced back at the sea, then said, 'Come inside. Let's get out of this cold.'

He held open the door and ushered her into the house but paused to take one last look at the night.

He didn't see Gabriel. He didn't see April. And he was already inside by the time the deep, gruff voices came drifting up from the water.

April heard them, though. Someone was down there. Someone was coming. But Gabriel was still crouched on the rooftop, and April didn't know if she should warn him or warn the strangers. She didn't know who she should trust. But it didn't make any difference, April remembered. The only person she could really count on was herself.

She just had to keep low. She just had to be quiet and careful and—

It didn't matter, because the next thing April knew, she was falling into the night.

Well, probably – technically – *falling* wasn't the right word.

It was more like sliding.

If you were on the World's Worst jungle gym.

April's butt was on the ground, and her legs were out in front of her. Her hands tried to stop her descent, but the more April clawed and kicked at the steep, rocky soil, the more noise she made, and the more noise she made, the more the men's shouts turned from '*What was that?*' to '*Who's out there?*'

When April finally crashed down on the rocky shoreline, her butt hurt and her hands burned, but April didn't dare make a whimper. She clung to the shadows and tried to stay still. She could hear the inky black water lapping up around a boat that was parked at the dock. She could see the silhouettes of the men who stood staring into the darkness, frozen in the act of carrying big wooden crates from the boat and down the dock and up the twisting stairs towards the house.

She didn't know who they were. She didn't know what they were doing. But something made her grateful that the moon had gone behind a cloud. They hadn't seen her. If she was quiet – if she was careful – she could slink away, down the shore and back to her hot shower and soft bed.

She didn't know who those men were or why Ms Nelson was there or what Gabriel planned to do with April's key, but none of it mattered right then, so she turned and started to run, but unfortunately for April, she ran right into a very hard, very broad, very smelly chest.

'Well, what do we have here?'

Strong hands gripped her arms, but this time they didn't belong to Gabriel Winterborne.

'Hey, boys,' the man yelled, 'we've got us a stowaway.'

Which didn't make any sense because April wasn't on the boat. But he pushed her towards the dock, and April

169

stumbled, falling hard. Her hand hit the water, and it was so cold. It was so dark. And April wanted to run, but when she looked back, she saw the gun.

'Move,' the man told her.

'Gladly,' a voice said.

And then something fell from the sky.

Except not *something*, April realised. *Someone.*

It all happened so fast. One moment, April was standing there terrified. The next, she was standing there mesmerised as Gabriel dropped on to the big man with the gun.

He turned to her and shouted, 'Run,' as another man rushed towards him. 'Now!' he yelled as he dodged and kicked, swerved and stabbed.

Yes. *Stabbed!*

Faint traces of moonlight flickered off of two shiny blades – a longer sword in his left hand and a shorter blade in his right. He used them both like they weren't just weapons, they were second limbs. Limbs that were sharp and strong and deadly.

One by one, the men fell or stumbled or ran back to the boat. He was too fast – too fluid. It was all too crazy. They were so confused and it was so dark and soon he was the only one left standing. He looked around, checking to see that the men on the ground were going to stay down.

And then his gaze flickered back towards the rocks, and April. 'Get out of here!' he called to her just as the boat roared to life, the engine loud in the darkness.

It charged down the length of the dock, shooting out to sea, and Gabriel was running after it, then diving on to the boat's deck as it pulled away.

He went for the man behind the controls first, and the boat slowed when Gabriel threw him across the deck, sending him crashing into the crates that went tumbling like a house of cards. One fell into the dark water with a splash. Gabriel turned at the sound, and that was his first mistake.

'Look out!' April couldn't help but shout when she saw another man moving towards him.

Especially once she saw the sword.

Gabriel must have dropped it at some point, because it didn't belong in the big man's hand. His motions weren't smooth, but the sword was very, very sharp. And Gabriel had turned too late.

He stumbled and looked down, almost insulted to see his own sword sticking out of his body as the men on the boat started closing in.

One of them took over the controls, and the boat shot off, water churning behind it in frosty waves, while Gabriel stood near the rail, looking between the dark water and the men and their crates.

April heard their laughter get fainter and fainter as the boat moved further and further down the shoreline. She wanted to scream again as she started to run, but the boat was too fast. The men were too strong. Mr Winterborne must have known it because he took another step. Then another. And another. And then he fell over the railing, splashing into the dark, freezing waters below.

SPAT OUT BY THE SEA. AGAIN.

Apdril ran until her lungs felt like they were going to burst. 'Come on,' she said to absolutely no one but the darkness. She was shaking, radiating with cold and fear, and so she didn't talk any more.

She screamed.

'Come on!'

The boat wasn't even a dot on the horizon, long since swallowed up by the night and the sea. The mini mansion was behind her, lost behind a curtain of fog. And April stood, looking out at the place where she thought he'd gone into the water.

'Gabriel . . .' The word was almost a sigh. 'Come on.'

Surely sword-wielding billionaires know how to swim, April thought. But just that quickly, she remembered black-and-white headlines and old grainy photographs – stories of a boy who had washed up on the rocky shore, alone and afraid, spat out by the sea.

She just had to hope that the sea would spit him out again. She hadn't found her mother yet. She needed her key. She was still mad at him but also grateful because he had just kinda sorta saved her life, and she kinda sorta felt like it might be her turn.

So she walked down the rocky shore, calling, 'Mr Winterborne!' even as a little voice in the back of her head whispered that he'd been in the water too long.

It was starting to look like maybe the ocean wanted him back.

April wasn't a very good swimmer, but she could doggy paddle and she could float.

She could fight.

When she saw something bobbing in the water, she ran into the waves, pushing against the current, screaming, 'Mr Winterborne!'

But absolutely no one shouted back, and when she realised the thing in the water was just the big, flat crate that had fallen overboard, she almost wept. But she didn't have time for weeping, so she yelled, 'Gabriel!' then threw an arm over the crate and kicked, trying to reach the place where she thought he'd gone in. She tried putting her head underwater, but it was too dark. It was too cold. She'd stopped shivering, and something told her that was a bad thing.

'Gabriel?' she whispered, like maybe the whole thing might have been a very bad dream.

She could feel her grip on the crate slipping, her hands too cold to hang on. The shore was too far away. Ms Nelson and Evert Winterborne might as well have been on another planet, and April knew she was on her own.

Like always.

Maybe it would be OK just to close my eyes for a little bit, a little voice inside of April said. *Maybe it would be OK just to let go of the crate.*

But something was shimmering in the distance. Like a mirage. Like that lady who lived in a lake – April thought someone was trying to give her a sword. Which seemed silly until she remembered: *sword.*

So April started kicking and praying and pushing the big crate until she reached the dark figure floating on the waves, the hilt of the sword still sticking out of the place where chest and shoulder meet.

'April.' His voice was faint, his face an eerie, ghostly white. Even as she reached for him, he seemed a million miles away. 'Save yourself.'

'No!' April shouted, pulling him closer. 'I'm gonna get us to the shore and then—'

'No. Just you, April.' He choked and gagged, the words ragged and as cold as the water. 'Only you.'

'No! I'm gonna get help. I'm—'

But then he surged, grabbing on to her with a power she didn't know he still had. 'Let me go, April,' he choked out. 'Let me go, and save yourself.'

'Please,' she begged as his arms went slack and his strength seemed to ebb away like the tide. 'Please don't leave me alone.'

'No one knows . . . alive. Can't tell. Secret.' His eyes fluttered closed, and the last word was nothing more than a ragged breath: '*Safe.*'

His grip softened. His head fell. Had she not heard his ragged breath, she would have sworn that he was dead. And, sadly, that wasn't their only problem.

The current was strong, and the fog was growing thicker by the moment. April was so turned around she didn't even know which way to kick. All around her, there was nothing but water, and for a moment all April could think about was what ten-year-old Gabriel must have felt the first time he washed ashore. Cold and lonely and afraid. But he hadn't died then, and he wasn't going to die now. April wasn't going to let the ocean win.

She just had to get him out of the water. She just had to get him warm. She just had to keep him from bleeding to death. But April was so cold and so tired.

'Wake up, Mr Winterborne.' Her teeth hurt as they rattled together. 'Please. You have to give me my key back. You have to tell me what it fits. You have to tell me what to do. I need you to wake up!' Then a cold, hard fact settled down on April, heavy enough that she was half afraid that it might sink them. '*I need you.*'

And then lights broke through the darkness: the shoreline, the cliffs and a mansion bright in the distance.

THE FAVOUR

'I need an invention.'

To Sadie's credit, she didn't look at April like she was crazy. It was more like she was . . . concerned. And intrigued. April couldn't blame her. After all, one and a half movies ago, April had been safe and warm and dry. And now April was . . . not. At all.

But there was also a not-quite-dead billionaire lying on the rocks with a sword sticking out of him, so April was trying really hard not to take it personally that Sadie was looking at her like maybe she was an experiment that had gone horribly, horribly wrong.

'Are you *wet?*' Sadie asked.

'Yeah. I—'

'Is that *seaweed?*' Sadie exclaimed, picking a piece of the long, stringy stuff off of April's black coat.

'I went for a swim,' April blurted when Sadie drew in a big breath as if getting ready to shout again.

Behind her, April could hear laughing and music. Light flickered through the crack in the doorway, and it was easy to imagine everyone snuggled up on couches with popcorn and fluffy blankets, waiting for the hero to save the day.

But April was proof that sometimes heroes end up half drowned and bleeding to death, needing heroines to do the heavy lifting.

And speaking of lifting . . .

'So about that invention—'

'Why would you go swimming? It's freezing out there. Or, well, not *technically* freezing. By my estimates, it's going to get down to one degree Celsius, but not until four a.m., and it's only—'

'Sadie!' April snapped. 'I need your help,' she said again, and Sadie grew serious, focused. She had a look in her eye like April was a problem that needed solving. And Sadie wasn't going to stop until she'd done it.

Behind April, a door must have opened and closed because, for one brief second, the hallway was bright, and Sadie's eyes went wide as she looked down at April's pale hands.

'Is that blood?'

'It's not mine,' April blurted.

'Is that supposed to make me feel better?'

'I wouldn't bother you.' April felt like she needed to say it quickly – get it all out before Gabriel died or she collapsed, whichever came first. 'But I really do need an invention.'

'What kind of invention?' Sadie asked.

April looked at her. 'The kind that can move a body.'

For a second, Sadie pondered that, as if 'body moving' might be a totally underserved segment of the invention-making market, but then she seemed to really hear what April was asking.

'I don't have . . . I don't make . . . I don't know how to move a body!'

Then April felt someone behind her. She turned to see Tim say, 'I do.'

April couldn't have been inside the mansion for more than ten minutes, but the fog was thicker and the sky was darker and everything felt different when she climbed down the

180

cliff than it had felt when she'd climbed up – probably because there was another set of feet crunching along behind her and a voice that kept saying, 'You know, we could go tell Ms Nelson.'

April shook her head and glanced behind her, grateful she'd thought to grab a torch when Tim went to get his coat.

'We can't.'

'Why not?'

Because he's been hiding from her for weeks. Because the last time I mentioned Gabriel Winterborne's name, she looked at me like I was a stain on her clean clothes. Because . . .

'Because we can't.' April skidded down the cliff and stood on the rocky shore for a minute, trying to get her bearings.

'OK. So where is this body?' He sounded sceptical, like he'd been thinking all along that April might be lying, but April didn't have the time or the energy to get angry.

Instead, she scanned the rocks and said, 'He's around here somewhere.'

'OK. Sure.'

'He is!'

'We could call 911,' Tim tried, but at that one, April had to laugh.

'Something funny?' Tim sounded more than a little offended.

'We can't call 911. He'd kill me.' She walked closer to the water.

'That's not making me think this is a good idea, you know.'

He might have had a point, but April didn't have time to care, so she threw up her hands and snapped, 'I don't mean *literally*. Or . . . well . . . I don't know. I just . . . Just help me get him back to the mansion and then you can forget all about it, OK? Forget about him and forget about me. Please.'

She turned and scanned the shore again, while Tim mumbled something that sounded a lot like, 'I can't forget about you,' but she couldn't be certain. It might have been the wind. It might have been her head. It didn't matter, though. Nothing mattered but finding Gabriel Winterborne.

She turned back to Tim, expecting scorn or ridicule or a fresh round of *let's-go-tell-a-grown-up*, but he just looked at her like he'd never seen her before.

'What?' she snapped.

'You said *please*.' Tim's voice was soft. 'You don't say please.'

'Yeah. Well. I'm saying it now.'

'What happened?' he asked.

Carefully, April turned again, shining her torch over the shore.

'He got beat up,' she said. They'd already lost too much time. Gabriel might have already lost too much blood. He might be too cold. Maybe Tim was right and they should call 911 . . . Maybe—

'Who is he?' Tim asked.

April didn't want to admit it, but if a guy is willing to climb a cliff and move a body, you kind of owe him the truth. So she said, 'Gabriel Winterborne,' and cocked an eyebrow, daring him to call her a liar.

There was a foghorn blowing in the distance. The water lapped against the rocks. But everything else was quiet as Tim stared at her. 'Look, I said I'll help you, but—'

'There!' April shouted as the torch's beam fell across a lump on the rocky ground.

His face was black and blue and swollen, but he

wasn't even trembling despite the cold. He wasn't doing anything. Maybe not even breathing. So when he groaned, it was the most wonderful sound April had ever heard.

'He's alive,' she sighed, sinking to her knees.

But Tim was shouting, 'There was a chance he *wasn't alive?*'

April whirled and gave Tim a grin. 'Yeah. Uh . . . he—'

'*Is that a sword?*' Tim gasped as the beam of April's torch caught on the shiny piece of silver sticking out of Mr Winterborne's shoulder.

'I thought I should leave it in until I could stop the bleeding.' She had been fairly proud of that decision, but Tim seemed to be stumbling over the whole *sword* aspect of the conversation.

'Sure. That's how I handle all my sword wounds.'

April was fairly certain he was mocking her.

She was even more certain she didn't care.

She leaned over Mr Winterborne and gently gripped the handle of the sword.

'I'm really sorry about this,' April said, then pulled it free. His whole body seized from the pain, but his eyes stayed closed and his chest kept rising and falling. When she got the torch, she'd also grabbed a towel from the bathroom, and now she pressed it against his wounds and tried not to think about the blood.

Some lights still burned in the mansion, but most of the windows were dark. They were alone as they stood looking up at the steep steps that crisscrossed their way up the cliff face. Gabriel Winterborne had probably climbed them a million times, but April and the other kids were strictly forbidden from those stairs. They weren't stable, Ms Nelson said. They were dangerous. People could get hurt.

Gabriel moaned.

People already were.

'I could go get help,' Tim said one more time, and April knew he wasn't wrong. But April's gut kept telling her he also wasn't right, even when he cast a worried look at the stairs. 'I don't think we can drag him up those.'

'We don't have to.'

She whistled, the sound piercing the air as the fog lifted. The clouds parted. And the moon shone down on Winterborne House like a spotlight as the small door that Gabriel had left through swung open. April was so glad Sadie had found it, especially when a rope fell down, complete with pulleys and hooks.

'Ready when you are!' Sadie yelled.

Tim looked like he didn't know whether to be impressed or terrified, but before he could say a word, Gabriel groaned again.

'Come on,' April said. 'We've got work to do.'

23

GABRIEL WINTERBORNE RETURNS

'Is he drunk?'

April had never seen Sadie's eyes get quite so wide or heard her voice sound quite so curious.

'No. Not drunk,' Tim said, dropping the sword to the cellar floor. It crashed and clanged, but April didn't care about the noise. Colin and Violet were surely in bed by then. Smithers was probably in the library with his nightly glass of port. Maybe Ms Nelson was back from Evert's and maybe she wasn't, but it felt like April, Tim and Sadie were the only three people in the universe. Four if you didn't forget the unconscious man. And April couldn't possibly forget about him.

None of them were even breathing hard, which meant Sadie could have a future in the body moving business, but now that Gabriel was back in his cellar, the problems seemed even bigger and bleaker and . . . well . . . bloodier than they had when he was lying on the rocks. Because getting him off the rocks was one thing. Keeping him alive was another.

'Here.' Sadie held up a lantern, sending soft yellow light across a mangled body.

His legs lay at a weird angle, and the bloody towel covered his chest. Had it not been for the ragged sounds his breath made, April might have thought that it was too late – that he was already dead. But he wasn't. And it was up to April to keep him that way.

'OK. We need something to disinfect the wound. And a needle and thread. Does Smithers have a first aid kit somewhere?' April looked up and, numbly, Sadie nodded.

'Great!' April pressed against the wound because they had to stop the bleeding. 'Great. I'll go—'

But Sadie was already saying, 'April, this man has been stabbed! We have to tell someone. He needs a hospital.'

'No!' April wasn't shouting. It was just that the cellar was super echoey and the mansion was too quiet. 'We can't tell anyone,' she said, calmer then.

On the crate, Gabriel winced and turned away from the light.

'He could die,' Sadie pleaded, because Sadie was rational. Sadie was smart and good and logical. So April needed a smart, good, logical reason why they shouldn't do the obvious thing.

'No. He won't. He can't die,' April said.

'How can you be so sure?' Sadie pleaded.

Then Tim brought the light closer to the face on the floor and said, 'Because he's already dead.'

'No.' Sadie started shaking her head. Or maybe she was just shaking. 'That's . . . This is . . . He's . . .' Then she looked around the dim, empty cellar and lowered her voice like she didn't want anyone to overhear. 'That's Gabriel Winterborne! You really found Gabriel Winterborne? You weren't—'

'No. I wasn't lying.'

'But *you found Gabriel Winterborne!* How? Where? How?'

April thought about the smoky museum and the way the dark figure had floated towards her like a dream. 'It's more like he found me. And then I tracked him down here.'

'When?' Tim asked, but April had the feeling it might have been a trick question. 'Was that why you were out wandering around that first night? Is that why you left Violet alone?'

But April didn't have time to deal with one mostly dead man and one half-angry boy. 'He was hungry. I started leaving him food and stuff.'

'Why didn't you tell us?' Sadie sounded hurt. But she wasn't bleeding, so Gabriel was still their biggest problem.

'He didn't want anyone to know he was back, OK? I don't know why, I just know—'

Sadie turned to Tim. 'We have to go get Smithers. Now!'

There's no way to know what would have happened next if a hand hadn't flown through the air and grabbed Sadie by the collar, pulling until she was face-to-face with the not-quite-dead man.

'Tell anyone I'm down here, and you'd better hope I die.' Gabriel's voice was raspy, but the words were clear, and Sadie's eyes were the size of dinner plates as she watched him drift out of consciousness, his knuckles still white on her shirt.

'See?' April said softly. 'He's been in hiding for ten

years. He's been down here for weeks. He could have walked upstairs anytime, but he didn't want Smithers to know. He didn't want Ms Nelson to know. *He was desperate that they not know.* I think he'd rather die than tell them. You want to trust a grown-up, right?' April asked, and Sadie nodded. 'Well, I do too. So I'm choosing to trust *him*.'

'But we can't let him die,' Sadie said one more time. 'We can't. We—'

'We won't.' Tim sounded so sure. 'He's not going to die.'

'You don't know that. The sword could have cut an artery,' Sadie said, but Tim was pulling back the towel. A little blood oozed out, but it wasn't flowing like it had been.

'April, did it bleed steady, or did it come out in bursts, like it was being pumped?' Tim asked.

April had to think for a moment. 'Steady.'

'Then it didn't hit a major artery. If it had, he would have been bleeding in time with his heartbeats. Besides . . .' Tim started but trailed off, rethinking whatever it was he was about to say. Which wasn't at all good enough for Sadie.

'*Besides what?*'

Tim shrugged. 'He'd be dead by now.' Tim pressed the towel back into place. 'So the stab wound won't kill him, but an infection could. And we have to warm him up. Slowly.'

'Tim, you don't know that,' Sadie said.

Tim was on the floor, balancing on the balls of his feet as he crouched over Mr Winterborne's body. He didn't look at Sadie as he said, 'You two are good at sneaking food and making inventions. I'm good at sewing up people no one wants to take to the hospital.'

'But how—' Sadie started.

He pulled back the collar of his shirt, and even in the dim light, April could make out the ragged line on his shoulder, not far from where Mr Winterborne's own scar would be. 'Knife.' Then he pulled up his jeans and pointed to the scars that covered his shins. 'Broken bottle.'

When he reached for his sleeve and started to reveal yet another story that April knew he didn't want to tell, she blurted, 'Tim, stop. You don't have to.'

He looked back at the man on the ground, and when he spoke, the words were low but heavy. 'Not everyone has a parent who's going to come looking for them, April.

Some of us hope we're never found.'

Then there was nothing but the sound of dripping water and the deep ragged breaths of the man who wasn't quite as dead as he wanted the world to believe.

'OK.' Sadie looked at Tim. 'What do we do?'

For the next hour, Sadie and April worked together while Tim went to get supplies. They had to cut off his coat, but his shirt practically fell apart under their touch, and Mr Winterborne moaned but didn't fight them at all, even though he must have been in terrible pain.

'I've never seen scars like that,' Sadie said at one point, but April had no idea which scars she was talking about — there were so many.

Tattoos ran in a line down his side, words April couldn't read. A puzzle she couldn't solve.

'What do you think they mean?' Sadie asked, but April just shook her head.

'I don't know.'

'Where was he all these years? Why did he come back now? What's he so afraid of?'

'I don't know.' April was shaking her head. She was so scared, but she couldn't say it — couldn't show it. She was still mad at him for breaking into their room and scaring

Violet and taking her key. But she was going to be way, way madder if he died.

So April let Tim douse him with alcohol, then carefully sew the wound. She watched as Sadie rigged up a heater and covered Mr Winterborne with blankets. Together, Tim and Sadie nailed big sheets of plastic over the parts of the cellar where the draughts were the worst.

But April . . . All April did was hold Mr Winterborne's hand.

And pray.

24

THE OTHER MR WINTERBORNE

'How is he?'

Things are supposed to look better in the morning – that's what people always said. But, in April's experience, people lied.

A lot.

'He's worse,' Sadie said even though the sun had come out and the air in the cellar felt crisp and clean, like new sheets on a perfectly made bed.

Things *should* have felt better.

But the man on the makeshift pallet was sweating and shivering at the same time, and no matter how many blankets they covered him with, he shook like he was still submerged in the icy water. No matter how many times they brought the wet sponge to his lips, he drank like he was lost in a desert.

No matter how many times April prayed for him to wake up and yell at her for bringing two more pesky kids into the sanctuary of his cellar, his eyes stayed closed, and his cries stayed muffled, and his fever never did break.

Luckily, it was Saturday, which meant no French lessons with Smithers or maths lessons with Ms Nelson, and as long as they took it in shifts, no one asked any questions – yet. They had time, April knew. She just hoped Gabriel Winterborne could say the same.

'He's not waking up,' Sadie said while she paced. 'Why hasn't he woken up?'

'His pulse is strong, and his colour is better,' April told her.

'But he's not waking up!' Sadie shouted, then seemed to feel bad about it. 'I'm sorry. I'm just worried.'

'I know,' April said. 'Me too.'

'It's just . . . That's *Gabriel Winterborne*. And I was raised that when you find a lost billionaire with a sword sticking out of him, you tell someone. Why is he here? Why didn't he tell anyone he was back? Why—'

'I don't know,' April said as Gabriel started tossing again. She tried to hold down his arm so he wouldn't tear his stitches, but he fought against her, mumbling, 'No. No. No!'

'Shh. It's OK,' April told him, because that's what mums always said in the movies.

'Have to move,' he said.

'No, actually, you have to stay very, very still,' April said, but he wasn't listening.

'Not safe. Never safe. Not safe. Never—'

The words were like a mantra – like a prayer – and when April told him, 'You're safe now,' he finally stopped fighting. But that was probably just because he was, once again, out cold.

'April?' Sadie asked after a long time. 'What happened last night?'

'I don't know,' April said again, but the truth was, she *did* know. Not everything. But she knew about a key and a trip to the mini mansion. She knew the way he'd crouched on the rooftop as the moon glistened off of his blades. She knew how he acted whenever he heard Ms Nelson's voice.

But, most of all, April knew he'd saved her. He'd saved her and then he'd told her to save herself and forget about him.

'April?' Sadie asked again.

'He stole my key,' April said before she lost her nerve. Her hand went to the place around her neck where it had hung ever since she could remember. 'That key I always wear . . . My mum left it when she left me. It's got the Winterborne crest on it, so I thought he could help me find whatever it opens. But he got real weird when I showed it to him, and then he broke into our room that night looking for it, and—'

'*He did what?*'

April hadn't heard Tim enter, but there he was, looking at her like lasers were going to start shooting out of his eyes.

'He . . . um . . .'

April tried to talk – really, she did. But Tim was pointing at the man on the ground and shouting, '*That's* who broke into your room?'

'I mean, technically, he owns the whole mansion, so does he ever have to' – she made quotation marks with her fingers – 'break in?'

'That man is dangerous,' Tim said, and April didn't know how to argue. 'He could have killed you.'

'Yeah, but he didn't, and then he saved—'

'*He could have hurt Violet!*' Tim shouted, because for him

198

that was the only point that mattered. Then he was heading back down the corridor from which he'd just come.

'Hey!' April called, but he didn't even slow down. 'Tim, wait.'

'No,' he shouted back. 'That man is dangerous, April. He could have hurt Violet. Or Sadie. Or you. He had a sword!'

'He wouldn't hurt me. He saved me!' April tried, but Tim didn't listen. 'Where are you going?'

'To do what I should have done last night!' Tim shouted back.

April knew she had to chase him down. Trip him. Tackle him. Pull a rug out from under his feet. She had to do something! Except a teeny-tiny voice in the back of April's head was whispering that maybe Tim was doing the right thing. Just for the wrong reason. After all . . .

Mr Winterborne was sick.

Mr Winterborne might be dying.

Mr Winterborne needed a hospital and medicine and help, so maybe April wasn't as fast as she could have been as she ran along in Tim's wake. So maybe April didn't do everything within her power to stop him as she followed him down the hall. Maybe she would have let him tell the world exactly who they had in the cellar except, in the next moment, the front doors flew open and Evert Winterborne yelled, 'Where is he?'

And then even Tim had to stop in his tracks. April and Sadie crept up behind him, peering over his shoulder as Smithers walked towards the open door.

'Mr Winterborne. How good of you to call.' Smithers's voice was still fancy and calm, but there was an underlying edge to the words. Then Evert pushed his way inside.

'Where is he?' Evert snapped, then looked around, as if expecting his nephew to pop out and yell *boo*. 'I know he's here somewhere. Where . . .' He started, then trailed off, and for a moment he just stood there, staring right at April – who had been caught by the men on Evert's pier. April, who had been rescued by the man with the swords.

It wasn't hard to do the maths. If Evert knew that Gabriel had been outside his house last night, then chances were he knew that April had been too. She waited for him to raise a finger and yell, *Trespasser!* But he didn't say a word to April. He just gave her a look that was sharper than Gabriel's sword and then he turned to Smithers.

His voice was like frost as he asked, 'Where is *Isabella?*'

And then Evert was off again, charging past Smithers

and down the hall, looking into every room. Tim started after him, but April grabbed his hand. 'Wait,' she said, and for a second, Tim froze, staring at the way her fingers wrapped around his. 'Please.'

'April—' Tim started, but there were footsteps on the stairs and Colin was grinning down at them.

'You've got to see this,' he said. A moment later, they were all rushing up the stairs and through the door and in between the dark shelves of books. Colin dropped to his stomach and crept towards the edge of the railing, silently looking down on where Ms Nelson was working below.

She was surrounded by a laptop and a half dozen newspapers and a notebook that was fatter than it should have been, bulging with Post-it notes and bits of paper sticking out from three sides. She looked as if the house could fall down around her and she wouldn't even notice. Maybe that was why she wasn't expecting the sound.

'There you are!'

Ms Nelson jolted when Evert pushed into the library, Smithers not far behind.

'Mr Winterborne to see you, Isabella.'

'Thank you, Smithers.' She smiled. She turned. And she, oh so casually, tucked that notebook beneath one of the newspapers before Evert got any closer.

'Where is he?' Evert snapped, looking around like Gabriel might be under the table.

'Who?' Ms Nelson asked.

'I know he's back, Isabella. And I know you're hiding him. Where's Gabriel?'

Even from the shadows of the second story, April could see all the colour drain from Ms Nelson's face. She actually looked unsteady as she rose to her feet. 'He's back?'

Gone were Evert Winterborne's comically large scissors and his sad eyes. He looked like a man being haunted by a ghost. 'If you're hiding him . . .'

She didn't answer. She laughed. 'Of course I'm not hiding him. Why would I ever . . . I want him found just as badly as you do. You know that.'

'Don't lie to me, Isabella. He's here. I know it. I can *feel* him.'

'So you'll call the judge, then?'

He looked confused. 'What—'

'If Gabriel's back, he's alive. And if he's alive, then you shouldn't get him declared dead, now, should you?' She raised an eyebrow, and the words might have been an arrow straight to his heart for how he reacted.

'I thought we were on the same side, my dear.'

'Of course we are.'

When he turned his gaze on her, she froze.

'You wouldn't lie to me, would you, Isabella?'

And at that, she finally smiled, but her voice and her eyes were cold. 'Don't you know, Evert? If Gabriel were back . . . I'd kill him myself.'

It was always hotter on the second story of the library, but that wasn't why April was sweating. She felt Tim shift beside her. She watched him start to push himself up from the floor.

'Tim?'

He froze, and for a second, their eyes locked and she could read his mind: five million dollars was a lot of money, but Tim would have handed over the man who broke into Violet's room for free.

Then, as if the thought had conjured her, Violet slipped through the doors and walked towards the banister where they all lay spying on the scene below. 'What's going on?'

'Shh, Vi,' Colin whispered. 'Come down here.' He reached for her hand, but it was suddenly shaking. Her sketchbook tumbled to the floor, fanning out, page after page of thick black crayon over white paper.

Page after page of the same thing: ruined bed curtains, broken windows and light glistening off a shiny silver blade.

'It's the Sentinel.' Violet's lip was trembling, but she didn't scream or back away. She just kept her gaze trained on the floor below.

Ms Nelson was walking Evert to the door, saying, 'You have my word. If we hear from Gabriel, you'll be our very first call.'

But up on the second floor, the kids were still and quiet, every eye locked on Violet as she pointed a finger at the man whose face she'd drawn on every page.

'That's him.'

April had no idea how long they sat there, surrounded by stillness and the weight of about a billion different secrets. But the silence must have been too much for Colin, who smirked and said, 'Well, I wonder what *that* was all about?'

But April knew. On instinct, her hand went to the place her key should have been, and she looked up at Tim. 'I was wrong. Gabriel didn't break in and steal my key . . .'

'It was Evert,' Tim filled in.

'Yeah. And if Evert's toting knives and breaking into rooms and stealing things . . . If he's hiring men with guns to do stuff in the middle of the night . . . Tim, if he's looking for Gabriel, then maybe . . .'

'You think Evert would hurt him?' Tim asked.

Sadie and April shared a look, and a cold chill seeped into April's bones as she glanced at Violet. 'I think he'd hurt *anyone*.'

'OK, *what is going on?*' Colin wasn't smiling any more.

But Sadie only whispered, 'You'll see.'

THE SHORT CON (ARTIST)

'So this is where you've been running off to.' Colin looked around the draughty cellar – at the arches on the ceiling and the passageways that branched off, going who knew where. He didn't seem at all concerned to have been led through a secret passageway and to a secret room with a very secret, very unconscious man on the floor. If anything, he only seemed upset that he hadn't been invited to the party sooner.

'So who's the almost dead guy?'

'Who do you think?' Sadie said, and Colin's eyes got wide.

'No way! You're putting me on.'

'Colin, Violet, meet Gabriel Winterborne,' April said.

'Is he sleeping?' Violet asked, looking up at Tim,

who hadn't wanted to bring her down but had been even more adamant about not leaving her alone.

'Yeah, Vi.' He tugged her closer. 'He's kind of sick, but we're gonna make him better.'

'How?' Sadie asked, because, really, that was the only thing that mattered.

Colin leaned over Gabriel's unconscious form, trying to get a better look. 'What's wrong with him?'

'Got stabbed with a sword, hit on the head, and thrown in the ocean,' April said simply.

'That'll do it.' Colin didn't bat an eye. 'Why's he down here?'

April could feel Tim's gaze fall on her. Sadie's too. And they weren't wrong. The longer Gabriel was unconscious, the thinner the ice they were all standing on became, and the truth was, it's one thing to tell a man you're willing to let him die. It's another to do it.

'He's hiding. We're hiding him. But he needs medicine, and we don't have any, so . . .' April trailed off, utterly unsure what came next.

She was expecting anything but the sight of Colin's shrug and the mumbled words, 'I can get you medicine.'

207

'You can?' Sadie asked, and Colin looked insulted.

'Love, have we met?'

'Dr Andrews? Smithers here, from Winterborne House. I believe we met at the hospital gala last – Yes, of course, doctor. So nice to hear from you as well.' The accent was smooth and cultured, rich and pure upper crust. The voice, on the other hand . . .

'My voice? Yes.' Colin coughed a little too loudly in April's opinion, but when the voice came again it was just right.

'I believe I've caught a bit of a bug. We've recently begun taking in . . . *orphans, you see*,' he said as if it were a dirty word befitting even dirtier children. 'Yes. I shudder to think what they might be bringing with them. I tell Ms Nelson they need a good delousing when they get here, but no one listens to me.'

Sadie threw out her hands in the universal signal for *isn't that a little much?* but Colin waved her away.

'Good of you to make time, my man, but I don't think there's any need to come in. I've had this before, and my London physician knew just what to give me. An antibiotic.' He looked down at the name of the drug that

Sadie had researched and read it off. 'Yeah. That'd be just the thing, you know. Just the thing.' He paused for a long time, and when he spoke again, his voice sounded even huffier. Almost like a warning. 'Excellent. Tell me, is there a pharmacy that delivers?'

And that was all it took. Just one eleven-year-old conman with a wider variety of British accents than anyone had realised, a 'borrowed' credit card, and a plan to distract Smithers as soon as the delivery van drew up to the house.

'Isn't that illegal?' Sadie asked.

'Yup,' Colin said.

'Then how did you know he'd go for it?' April asked, and Colin looked at her like she might be the most naive girl in the world.

'Winterborne House means money. Money means it's just a phone call away.'

'You mean *it* like medicine?' April asked.

Colin shook his head. '*It* like anything.'

April had stolen a lot of things in her twelve years: food from locked pantries, a pair of shoes from the lost and found, once even a puppy for a whole afternoon because it was cold outside and no one seemed to care how much the poor thing kept shivering.

But listening to Colin, April wondered for the first time if it might be possible to steal another life.

Sadie calculated the dose, and then they changed Mr Winterborne's bandages and brought down some fresh blankets.

And then they waited.

MS NELSON'S SECRET(S)

FROM THE RECORDS OF SADIE MARIE SIMMONS

9:38 p.m. The Patient exhibits sensitivity to light, noises and Colin's 'talent' on the harmonica.

11:45 p.m. The Patient seems to be thirstier. And sweatier. And stinkier. He is also, luckily, no deader than he was.

2:22 a.m. The Patient has grown more restless and is mumbling in his sleep. So far we've learned ten new curse words. (We think. We just don't know what language they are or what they mean yet.)

5:15 a.m. The Patient isn't sweating any more, and he feels cooler to the touch.

8:45 a.m. The Patient's fever has broken, but

he hasn't woken up yet.

11:00 a.m. No change.

2:00 p.m. No change.

6:00 p.m. No change.

'How's he doing?' April asked as soon as she reached the room they'd made for Gabriel. It was still a damp, creepy cellar, but it seemed homier somehow.

There were lights now and pillows and a camp bed. A table with water and an ice chest filled with juice boxes. Someone had dragged in some folding chairs and a couple of laptops. It was like a real room in a real house, for a real family. Which made sense, April supposed. Kids like them were used to making homes out of anything – anywhere. She shouldn't have been surprised they'd done it there.

'He's better,' Sadie said. 'I think. The fever hasn't come back, and his pulse seems stronger, and his colour's better. But . . .'

'He still hasn't woken up,' April finished.

Sadie shook her head then glanced at Colin, and when she spoke again, her voice was timid and soft, and April didn't like the sound of that one bit. 'You don't really think Ms Nelson meant it, do you? When she said she'd kill him herself?'

April had been playing that scene over and over in her mind all day, but she still had to think about the answer.

'No. I don't think she'd kill him. But she could tell Evert, and . . .' April hesitated. 'What if that's the same thing? I mean, he broke into our room, and . . . I don't like him.'

She looked at Colin, who shrugged. 'Uncle Evert gives me the creeps, and I was raised by professional criminals.'

'I don't like him either,' Sadie admitted. 'But maybe she wouldn't tell Evert?'

But April was shaking her head. 'She was there. At Evert's house. When this happened.' April pointed down at Gabriel and the wound that had only barely started to heal. 'Ms Nelson was there. Meeting with Evert. While creepy dudes with guns did stuff under the cover of darkness and Gabriel skulked around with a sword. There's just so much we don't know!'

'OK. It's just that . . .' Sadie and Colin shared a guilty look. Like they'd been up to something.

'What?' April asked.

'We translated his tattoos.' Sadie led her to the far side of the room where they'd set up the table and the laptops. 'It was easy, really, once we identified the languages. There are six. Hindi. Korean. Chinese. Spanish. Arabic. And Russian.'

'*Okaayyy*,' April said, drawing out the word. 'What do they say?'

'See this?' Colin pointed at a long string of numbers. 'That's an international phone number. As for the rest, well, that's just it. They all say the same thing – the exact same thing,' Colin told her, then nodded at Sadie, as if he was willing to let her have the good part.

'They all say "*If I'm dead, tell Izzy I'm sorry.*"'

For a long moment, there was no sound in the cellar. It seemed like the critters stopped scurrying and the water stopped dripping and even their hearts stopped beating.

'Sorry for what?' April asked.

Sadie shrugged. 'Something bad enough that he'd rather die down here than live up there.'

April thought about the woman upstairs and the man on the floor, but it felt like an ocean still stood between them. Well, two storeys, several tonnes of stone, a very dusty passageway, five kids and one really big secret.

'I get where you're coming from – I really do,' Sadie said. 'But I also don't want to go upstairs in a day or two and tell her he's dead, but – don't worry – he's also super sorry about it. Do you want to tell her that?'

'No. But—'

'She's hiding something,' Colin filled in.

Sadie looked at him like he was crazy. 'This is Ms Nelson! We know her. We know—'

'She has secrets. Don't give me that look, Sade. *Everyone* has secrets.' He said like it was the most obvious thing in the world.

'Like what?' Sadie crossed her arms.

'Like this.'

April hadn't really meant to steal the notebook. She'd only thought about borrowing it. Maybe taking a glimpse. Maybe a peek. Maybe . . .

'How'd you get that?' Sadie asked.

April shrugged. 'It was in the library. We're allowed to take books out of the library, right?'

The rule absolutely, positively didn't mean they could take Ms Nelson's personal journal without her permission, but desperate times called for desperate measures.

She saw Violet and Tim enter the room, and Tim

froze at the sight.

'Is that . . .'

'Ms Nelson's planner? Yes.' Colin was already reaching for it.

'We shouldn't have that,' Sadie said.

'You saw her slide it out of sight.' Colin opened up the book. 'Don't you want to know what she's hiding from ol' Evert? Because I, for one . . . Hey! I was looking at . . .'

But Colin trailed off when, suddenly, the book was in Sadie's hands and Sadie's hands were starting to shake.

'That's my mum and dad.' Sadie looked down at a newspaper article pasted on the very first page. **WINTERBORNE DEVELOPERS DIE IN FATAL COLLISION**. 'Why does she have an article about my mum and dad?'

'I don't know,' April said.

Colin took the book back and started flipping through the pages. There were handwritten notes that didn't make any sense – maps with points circled and long lists of places and dates. It was like the scrapbooks Smithers kept in the library. But different. The book bulged with newspaper clippings from all over the world – in languages April couldn't read.

There were questions and charts and two whole pages

covered with just four words: *Where are you, Gabriel?*

'She's been looking for him,' Colin said as he ran a finger over the pages. Then he stopped flipping as Tim touched a page and stared down at the headline CONVICTED FELON WASHES ASHORE, FOUL PLAY SUSPECTED.

'Tim?' April asked, because he was staring down at a mug shot on the page. 'Are you OK?'

'That's my dad.' His voice sounded too small in the big room. 'So I guess he's dead now. That's good to know.'

He walked away like he didn't want to touch the book any more, and April looked down at the clipping that was already turning yellow with age. There was no date, but it had obviously been there long before Tim came to Winterborne House – long before Ms Nelson oh so casually asked him to tag along with Violet.

'See?' Colin cocked an eyebrow at Sadie. 'Secrets.'

When he started thumbing through the book again, something fell out. No. Some *things*, April realised as she looked down at a floor littered with pretty pictures of faraway places.

'Are those postcards?' Sadie asked as April picked them up, then turned them over and over in her hands, knowing they must matter.

Athens. Oslo. Tokyo. Dubai. Egypt. Norway. Dubai.

She read them once. Then twice. They were blank on the back – nothing but the address to Winterborne House and their postmarks.

'Athens. Oslo. Tokyo. Dubai. Egypt. Norway. Dubai,' Sadie rattled off as April laid the postcards out one by one.

'Why have both Oslo and Norway?' Sadie asked.

'And why are there two from Dubai?' April said the only thing that stood out to her. 'It's the exact same postcard but they were sent months apart. Why . . .'

It was Violet who finally said, 'Put them in order,' then took the cards and rearranged them according to the dates on the postmarks, fanning them out until only the first letter of each card was visible – the message as clear as day.

NOT DEAD.

'What can I say?' a deep, gravelly voice said from behind them. 'I always did like puzzles.'

DEAD MEN DO TELL TALES

Gabriel Winterborne was still alive, but he looked half dead as he leaned against the cellar wall. He wore a blanket around his shoulders and held it tight, as if he could keep his scars and tattoos hidden from the kids who had already seen and heard too much.

'Hello, April.' His voice was deeper, rougher, but his eyes held a mixture of disappointment and wry amusement – like he didn't know whether he should be happy or sad to have . . . you know . . . *not died*. Which was the most Gabriel Winterborne-y thing that April had ever seen.

'I suppose you don't understand the meaning of the words *don't tell anyone*.'

'You were dying,' she said. 'And besides, you're heavy.'

Sadie studied Mr Winterborne, probably trying to guess

what his temperature and blood pressure might be. Colin looked like it was a pity they didn't have popcorn. But Tim was the one who looked like April felt: like he knew a conscious Gabriel Winterborne might be scarier than the man on the pallet any day. So he pulled Violet closer. And waited.

'Mr Winterborne.' Sadie inched forward, deadly serious. 'I'm Sadie—'

'I know,' he snapped. 'You're Dr Simmons's daughter.' He looked at Colin. 'And you're the con artist's kid. And you . . .' He trailed off when he looked at Tim. 'You're the son of the man who tried to kill me.' Mr Winterborne finished with a shrug. 'Or *one* of them.'

'Did you kill him?' Tim asked.

Slowly, Gabriel shook his head. 'Wrong Winterborne. If you haven't learned by now, Uncle Evert doesn't leave loose ends.'

April gulped and thought about the shady men she'd seen doing shady things on the dark dock. She remembered the way Evert had looked at her after – like she was a mess he'd have to clean up eventually. But that was Future April's problem. Present April had a half-dead billionaire and a roommate who wasn't bouncing any more.

'Mr Winterborne?' Sadie's voice wasn't as strong as it usually was. 'There were some other articles . . . about . . .'

'I'm sorry, Sadie. Your mother and father were brilliant people. They didn't deserve to die. But neither do most of the people who die in my place.'

'No. See . . . they had an accident.' Her voice cracked as she pleaded, 'It was an *accident*. Wasn't it?'

But Gabriel was shaking his head. 'I can't be sure. I was gone by then, but . . . your dad designed the ship. Did you know?' he asked, but didn't wait for an answer. 'Publicly, Evert blamed your father. Ruined his career – labelled him "the man whose negligence killed the Winterbornes". But of course, privately, we all knew why the boat sank.'

'Why did it sink?' Colin asked, and Gabriel raised an eyebrow.

'Because bombs and boats don't mix.'

'But that doesn't make any sense,' Sadie said, and April couldn't blame her. Sadie's was a world of science. Where equations always balanced and actions had equal and opposite reactions. 'If there was a bomb, my dad would have proven it. There would have been investigations. It would—'

'*Oh*. I wish we'd thought of that,' Gabriel said

221

drily. 'But I seem to remember the evidence being at the bottom of the ocean and people not being willing to take the word of a ten-year-old boy, a disgraced engineer and a butler.'

Then the work of standing upright seemed too much for him and he staggered to the table and downed a bottle of water in one long gulp. He looked frail and weak, and April couldn't help but think about the tattoos and the woman right upstairs.

'Do you want me to go get Ms Nelson? Or Smithers?'

'No!' he snapped, then leant against the table. 'The element of surprise is all I have, and I won't let you take it away from me.'

'Evert's trying to have you declared dead,' April said.

Gabriel huffed. 'Good. Maybe then he'll stop trying to kill me.'

'But you're alive,' April said.

'Doesn't feel like it.'

'But if you tell people you're back, then—'

'Who are you going to tell, little girl?' Gabriel snapped. 'Who is going to listen to a handful of orphans and a dead man?'

'Well,' Sadie said in her most scientific voice, 'when the

man in question is demonstrably *not dead*, it would be—'

'Do you think I haven't tried?' Gabriel's words echoed around the room.

'When I was ten, I washed up on the shore. When I was twelve, I started having *accidents*. Luckily, my parents' will gave Smithers custody. He brought on Izzy's father to lead my security detail, and I was safe. For a while. But I was the only thing standing between my uncle and the Winterborne *legacy*, as he liked to call it. I was rich and famous and privileged beyond compare, and no one beyond this house believed a word I said. But go on. Be my guest.'

He poured water on a rag and wiped his face. 'Maybe they'll listen to you. They never listened to me.'

He turned back to them, finished with his lecture. But the story wasn't over, of that much April was sure.

'Mr Winterborne?'

'Don't call me that!' Gabriel shouted, then seemed to feel badly about it. '*He's* Mr Winterborne. Not me. Never me.'

'OK. Um . . . Gabriel? What happened when you were twenty-one?'

'My uncle tried to kill me.' He raised an eyebrow, then

223

gave a quick, cold laugh. 'Again.'

'You might as well just tell the whole story, you know? They won't leave till they hear it,' Tim said, and Gabriel looked at him like he might be the only one of them who had any sense, and then he started to talk.

'On my twenty-first birthday, I was going to come into my inheritance – take over the business. Become a man.' He huffed, then winced in pain from the effort. 'But I was still a boy, really. Arrogant. I told my security I didn't need them any more. I said I was the head of Winterborne Industries now, and I didn't need a babysitter. Izzy . . . Izzy told me I was stupid – that something bad was going to happen, and I'd deserve it. She was right.

'I didn't see your father.' He looked at Tim. 'Not at first. He hit me on the back of the head and knocked me to the ground. Then he took my wallet and my father's watch. It had been in the shop when the ship sank, so I had it. I always wore it. For a second, I actually thought that maybe it really was just a robbery. But then he had a gun, and . . .

'It didn't hurt at first. Because of the adrenaline, I guess. I fell into the water and stayed under. Swam as far as I could. When I came up for air, I heard shouting and sirens, and I knew he was probably gone. But I also knew he'd come back.' He levelled April with a glare. 'Him or others just like him. They would *keep coming back.*'

For a long time, April and the others stayed silent – unwilling or just unable to break the spell, waiting for Gabriel to finish. 'I managed to climb aboard one of the ships, and then I just . . . went away.'

'Just like that?' Colin sounded doubtful. 'You. Gabriel Winterborne. Just floated off into the sunset? Just like *that?*' Colin snapped his fingers, and Gabriel shrugged.

'Izzy and I used to joke about it – what if we ran away? What if we moved to the other side of the world? What if . . . I don't think she really thought I'd do it. Not without her. But Evert would have kept trying until I was dead. Until *everyone I loved* was dead. So I decided to just *be* dead.'

He took a ragged breath, and April knew that the question was no longer why he'd run. The question was . . .

'What do we do now?' Sadie said.

Gabriel looked like he would have laughed if he'd had the energy. '*We?*'

'Yeah. You need us!' Colin said. 'We're . . . you know . . . *not dead.*'

'You will be if you don't leave me alone,' Gabriel

said, and April knew words wouldn't convince him. There were no facts, no figures, that could have possibly changed his mind.

So April punched him in the shoulder.

'Ow!'

He recoiled even though she hadn't even punched him very hard. Really, Violet hit way harder in her sleep.

'What was that for?' he cried.

'To show that you need us. You might as well go ahead and let us help. We're precocious.'

'I have other words for you,' Gabriel grumbled, but he looked around at them, the children who had saved his life. 'Go to bed. All of you.' He stumbled to the pallet and dropped to his knees. 'I'm sure I'll see you in the morning.'

April couldn't sleep. She didn't even try. She just lay in her big, soft bed, staring up at the Winterborne crest woven into the canopy overhead, thinking about long-lost billionaires and murderous uncles. She'd spent her whole life wondering who her family might be, but now she wondered if maybe families might be overrated. At least if they didn't know you, they couldn't try to kill you. That had to be a good thing, right?

Then, for about the nine billionth time, April reached for her key and came up empty-handed. The wind howled outside, and she wondered if Gabriel was warm enough down in the cellar. Did he have enough water? What if the fever came back? But mostly she thought about what he'd told them. And she knew that his body was going to heal, but she wondered if the rest of him would ever do the same.

'April?'

When the voice came through the darkness, April wasn't surprised to hear it. There had been the same tossing and turning coming from the other side of the room for hours, even after Violet drifted off to sleep.

'Yeah?' April asked.

'Do you think Evert killed my parents?'

It wasn't hard to imagine Sadie running those data points through her mind over and over, looking for a way that two plus two could somehow equal fifty.

'I don't know,' April said.

A tree limb scratched against the brand-new window, and the house seemed to creak and moan under the weight of all that stone and wood.

'April?'

'Yeah?'

'I'm sorry I didn't believe you – when you said you'd found Gabriel Winterborne. I should have listened. I'm sorry.'

'That's OK,' April said, because it was. No one ever believed April. She hadn't really expected the people at Winterborne House to be any different.

'April?' Sadie's voice was softer this time, as if she was already half asleep.

'Yeah?'

'We're gonna get your key back.' Sadie yawned. 'I promise.'

Promises were easy to make and hard to keep, but April closed her eyes and didn't say so. She just lay there for a long time, listening to the wind.

THE FORGOTTEN ROOM

'I'm awake!'

April didn't mean to shout. Or to knock a notebook, two pens, and a glass of water off the table. She absolutely, positively did not intend to drool. But that's exactly what happened as Ms Nelson stood in front of the class the next afternoon, a very confused/amused/disappointed look upon her face.

'April, perhaps you can explain why plants always lean towards the light?'

April glanced at Sadie, expecting the answer to come bursting out of her like a burp or a sneeze. But Sadie was silent. Sadie was still. And April didn't know whether to be worried or comforted by the fact that even Sadie was still lost in a fog about all they'd seen and heard the night before.

But, mainly, April couldn't stop looking at Ms Nelson and wondering, *What else are you keeping from us?*

'What's wrong with everybody? Do you guys have a case of the Mondays?' Ms Nelson teased. She laughed. She hadn't yet figured out that she was surrounded by children who didn't quite trust her any more.

'April?'

And then she was saved by a knock on the door.

'Excuse me, Isabella.' Smithers peeked into the schoolroom. 'The real estate agent is calling for you.'

'Thank you, Smithers,' she said, then started for the hall. 'Let's get back to this tomorrow, shall we? I think we all need a night off.'

She gave a quick glance back at the group. But she didn't say anything before leaving the kids to their secrets and their silence.

'So what happens now?' Sadie could have been talking about life without classes or the billionaire in the basement, but the answer seemed to be the same either way because they kept on sitting there, doing nothing.

Then there was singing. Or humming. Or something in between as Smithers swept into the room and started

230

tidying up the bookshelves.

'Smithers?' Colin said. 'Why's Ms Nelson talking to a real estate agent?'

It took Smithers a suspiciously long time to reply, 'She's looking at houses.'

'Why?' Tim asked, and Smithers considered his words carefully.

'Because this house belongs to the Winterborne family – not the foundation – so we may be moving soon.'

'Why?' This time it was Violet, and that stopped Smithers in his tracks.

'Because in a couple of weeks, a judge will most likely declare Gabriel Winterborne legally dead. It's been ten years, and the courts believe . . . That is to say . . . Evert has tried . . .' Smithers started and stopped until he finally settled on, 'We may be moving to a new house!' and then he went back to work and, if possible, the room got even quieter.

So Colin pushed away from the table and mouthed the words *come on*.

'No one'll find us in here.'

As soon as Colin opened the big double doors, April

231

believed him. She almost choked, the dust was so thick and the air was so stale. She wanted to throw open the windows and let in the cool ocean breeze, but she knew somehow that was a bad idea.

'Colin . . .' Sadie's voice was a warning. 'I thought this room was locked?'

'It was.' He winked. 'Now it's not.'

If April had still believed in ghosts, she might have worried because it looked like a family of them lived there. Huge sheets hung over every piece of furniture. They'd probably been white, once upon a time, but now the whole room was dingy and grey. Like a castle in a movie that had been asleep for decades.

'You sure Smithers won't find us in here?' Tim asked.

Colin laughed. 'Does it look like Smithers spends a lot of time in here?'

With that, he jumped on to the bed, a thick cloud of dust billowing out when he landed.

Tim pulled back the thick velvet drapes, revealing a whole wall full of windows overlooking the cliffs and the sea. It was the prettiest view in a house full of beautiful views, and April turned.

'Colin, what room is this?' she asked just as Violet

tugged on one of the sheets, revealing a painting like the ones in the museum. But different. In this one, a ten-year-old Gabriel was sitting on the floor by his parents' feet, surrounded by his brothers and sisters, all of them smiling and laughing and happy.

April looked around the room again. There were clothes in the closets. Two toothbrushes in the bathroom. A pair of high-heeled shoes lay discarded by the bed. It wasn't hard to imagine a grief-stricken ten-year-old ordering that his parents' room be boarded up like a capsule. And now, even twenty years later, it was still frozen in time, waiting for a ship that was never going to make it back to shore.

'Like I said.' Colin shrugged. 'No one's gonna come looking in this room.'

There were framed photographs on every surface. Kids playing in the water. A man and woman in love. A family gathered around a Christmas tree, all of them – even Smithers – in ugly sweaters. Well . . . everyone except Evert, who stood awkwardly behind them in his dark suit, glaring at the camera.

The dust danced in the light that streamed through the windows, and when Sadie spoke, she sounded different than April had ever heard her. 'OK, April, tell us everything.'

'Me? I don't know anything!'

'We know why Colin's here. And me. And Tim. And presumably Violet's here because of Tim,' Sadie went on. 'But there's nothing in Ms Nelson's notebook about you, so haven't you wondered why *you're* here?'

April hadn't wondered, actually. 'I just assumed someone called her. I mean, she's the head of the Winterborne Foundation, right? So they would have told her about the fire. And about me. I didn't think too much about it. Ms Nelson was just there when I woke up in the hospital, and—'

'You were in the hospital?' Sadie's voice was too loud, and April was suddenly grateful for the sheer size of Winterborne House.

'Yeah. I sort of . . . um . . . burned down the museum.'

'You burned down the museum?' If possible, Sadie's cry was even louder.

'It wasn't a big deal.' (*It was totally a big deal.*) 'I thought my key might open a box in the Winterborne collection, but it didn't. And then I knocked over a candle, and the whole place went . . . *poof*. I didn't mean to! It just happened so fast. And . . .'

For some reason, April didn't want to tell them about being saved by a Gabriel Winterborne-shaped figure – about the way her key tumbled out of her hands and then ended up back around her neck.

'Why should I be in the book? The fire was the night before she got me. No one ever cared about me before then. And I never told *anyone* about my key. Not until Evert broke in here and stole it.'

'We have to get Gabriel to go public,' Sadie said.

But Colin only laughed. 'Good luck with that, love. You might find out if he's got a bite to go with that growl.'

'Wouldn't help anyway,' Tim added.

'Why not?' Sadie asked.

'Because a Dead Gabriel isn't our problem. A Live Evert is.'

Tim wasn't suggesting they kill him.

Probably.

Almost definitely.

Surely Tim wasn't suggesting they kill him? April wondered, but Sadie was looking at him like she wouldn't rule anything out.

'So how *do* we stop Evert?' Sadie asked. 'What are his weaknesses? What does he want? What—'

'My key.' April's hand went to her neck again and came up empty. Again. 'He broke into our room to take it. So it must be important.'

'What does it open?' Violet sounded so young when she said it. It wasn't her fault. She didn't know that was the question that had pretty much dominated April's entire life and she still didn't have any answers.

'I don't know,' April admitted.

'How'd you get it?' Tim asked.

'My mum. She left it when she . . . when she left me. And before you ask, no. I don't know who she is. I don't know where she is. I don't know how she got it or why or when, but I know Evert was willing to break in here to steal it. So I know that Evert must need it.'

'No, love.' Colin shook his head. His eyes twinkled. 'He needs whatever is behind the lock that that key opens.'

April thought about her first morning at Winterborne House – about how she'd been nervous and tired and covered in porridge when Evert just appeared in the corridor after everyone had thought he'd gone home.

'Sadie, remember when you told me that Evert shows up here sometimes and wanders around?' April asked, and Sadie nodded. 'What if he's been looking for something?'

'Like what?' Sadie asked.

'I don't know. But Colin's right. Evert needs something that's locked up in this house. And if he needs it . . .' April trailed off, and Tim finished.

'So do we.'

April was out of breath when they finally reached the cellar, but she still managed to blurt out, 'What does it open?'

'Hello to you too,' Gabriel said, looking around at the group. 'I'm still alive, as you can see. A little hungry. Perhaps—'

'Evert broke into our room and stole my key. He risked us seeing him or being caught by Smithers and Ms Nelson. Why?'

'Because it's pretty? Because it drove him crazy to see our illustrious family crest around the neck of an orphan? Because he's insane? Take your pick,' Gabriel said. 'It's not like it matters.'

'But what if it does?' Sadie asked. 'If we could get April's key—'

'And how exactly are you going to do that?' Gabriel challenged, and at first, Sadie recoiled a little, but then she grew braver. 'We're gonna steal it.'

'Yeah!' Colin cried out. 'Now we're talking.'

'No! I can't keep all of you safe if you go—' But he stopped when he realised April was actually, literally, laughing at him. 'Something funny?'

'We don't need you to keep us safe. I don't even need you to get into Evert's house. I can climb up, shimmy through a window and—'

'No!' Gabriel's shout echoed around the big stone room, and when he leaned down, she could look into his eyes, past the pain and the sorrow. She saw the little boy from the paintings, and she remembered that Gabriel Winterborne had been sharpening his swords since he was ten years old.

'That man killed my entire family – *his* entire family. So tell me this . . . What do you think he'd do to the likes of you?' The words weren't a threat. They were a warning.

But April had already seen Evert's men working on the dock. April had already worn Evert's precious key around her neck for years. April and the other kids were already in too deep, and as far as April could tell, they had two options: drown or start swimming. So she didn't have time to be afraid.

'You don't get it, Gabriel . . .' April said. 'I never had a family. I'm not afraid of yours.'

'He's dangerous!'

'So are you,' April told him. 'And you're not alone any more.'

HOW TO STOP AN EVIL UNCLE
IN THREE EASY STEPS

TO DO LIST:

1. Get key.
2. Find lock.
3. Win.

That was it. It was just that simple. But, sadly, simple didn't always equal easy. Because Winterborne House was still huge. And Gabriel was still surly. And at the end of the day, they still didn't know how to get the key or where to find the lock, and 'winning' depended entirely on what Evil Uncle Evert was so desperate to get his hands on. Plus, it was a concept that April didn't have a lot of experience with. But there was a first time for everything. Or so she told herself.

So instead of focusing on the things she didn't know, she decided to focus on the things she did. Like how Sadie Marie Simmons was, in fact, a genius, and how if Violet stood on a chair and screamed, 'Mouse!' at the top of her lungs, Smithers and Ms Nelson would both be distracted for at least an hour.

She thought about the ten jewellery boxes, nine music boxes, and four wall safes they'd found – not to mention the three abandoned suites in the family wing that you could access via secret passage.

And, finally, April remembered that even though most people feel better once they start sleeping in real beds, eating real food, and taking real showers, Gabriel Winterborne was not most people.

'April!'

The shout echoed off the stone walls and hard floor, and April had to wince. And force a smile. And remind herself that she'd spent days hoping he would wake up, so it would be wrong for her to wish him unconscious again. Very wrong. So, so wrong. But April did it anyway, because Fever Gabriel never yelled, and in that sense, he was April's favourite Gabriel by far.

'What is all this?'

The floor was covered with cords and cables. TVs leaned against the wall while Colin stood atop a ladder, a cordless drill in his hands and a very Sadie-ish gleam in his eye.

'Did you have a nice shower?' April asked. His hair was wet, and his clothes were clean, and April had thought he'd be in a good mood when he got back from the bathroom in the family wing where they'd left not one, not two, but *three* kinds of bubble bath and a brand-new razor (which he hadn't even used). But instead he was pointing at the screens that Tim and Colin were mounting on the wall.

'What are those?'

'Monitors,' April said simply.

'Why are there *monitors* in my cellar?'

'Because it turns out Evil Uncle Evert uses the same security system as Winterborne House, and Sadie was able to hijack the feed. That way we can keep an eye on him from a distance because, as you like to remind me, *we're just kids*. Or would you prefer *not* to have eyes on your murderous uncle?' When he didn't answer, she had to smirk. 'That's what I thought.'

'Aren't you worried Smithers will come looking for you?'

Colin hopped down from the ladder. 'Oh, he's watching that British cooking show he's so into. It's trifle night. The house could burn down, and he wouldn't notice on trifle night. But just to be safe, Violet's keeping a lookout.'

'And what about . . .' He couldn't even say the word *Isabella*.

'She left an hour ago,' Tim said.

'She's looking for a new house,' April added. 'For us to move into. *When you're dead.*'

Gabriel probably didn't even realise he was glancing towards his swords. And the cliffs. But he was winded just from going to take a shower. He had no business tracking Ms Nelson – not when he couldn't even keep himself safe at the moment.

When he said, 'You shouldn't be doing this,' he didn't even sound angry any more. Not even disappointed. He just looked . . . sad.

'We want to do this,' April told him.

'No. You don't know what you're getting into.'

'Do I need to remind you who it was who dragged you out of the water and saved your life?' April asked.

'I wouldn't have been in the water if you hadn't been there! I would have . . .'

'What?' April asked. 'What would you have done?'

Then, for the first time since April had known him, Gabriel Winterborne looked guilty.

'I wouldn't have had to save you.'

She didn't say what she was thinking: that he'd needed saving a long time before he went into the water.

He walked to the other side of the cellar and the narrow bed they'd found in the attic. He pushed aside the stack of clean clothes Colin had pilfered from the things Smithers was going to give to charity. He didn't look all that happy to be wearing a T-shirt that said BUTLERS BUTTLE BETTER. It was too small and pulled tight across his chest, but it was soft and clean, and he didn't complain as he pulled an old threadbare sweater on over that and tossed his towel over the back of a chair.

He looked grumpy, and April couldn't entirely blame him. After all, in the two days since he'd woken up, his very quiet, very dull cellar had become . . . crowded.

Half of Sadie's lab had been moved to one of the passageways. Tim and Violet had found a doll's house that looked exactly like Winterborne House, and they'd turned it into a model of the mini mansion, complete with stickers for cameras and action figures for guards.

The dark and dirty cellar was part lab, part playroom, part bedroom, part . . . home.

But that was before the explosion.

'What in the . . .' he shouted as dust fell from the ceiling and the cellar shook. Smoke filled the air as Sadie emerged from the haze.

Her hair was sticking up, and dust covered her face, and she was shouting, 'I'm OK!' a little too loudly – like her ears weren't working right.

'Are you sure? Your hair is kind of . . . smoking,' Colin said, patting one of Sadie's signature topknots.

But Sadie just grinned and shouted, 'I got it!'

'Got what?' Colin sounded concerned as a low hum filled the air. Then there was movement on one of the monitors, and April realised that it wasn't showing the feed from Evert's security system. It was showing the feed from . . .

April looked up and saw a drone the size of a shoebox hovering overhead.

'I call it the SadieSeer 200!'

Sure enough, SADIESEER 200 was painted right on the

side in big white letters.

'Uh, maybe don't put your name on the thing that we're going to use to plan a heist?' Colin told her.

Sadie considered it for a second, then nodded. 'Good note, Colin!' She used the remote, and soon the drone was dropping down and hovering right in front of the group. 'It has a three-hundred-and-sixty-degree rotating camera. Night vision. A two-mile range, and . . . uh . . . let's call it stealth mode.'

'Stealth mode?' Tim asked.

'Yeah. I can make it . . . uh . . . explode. Just a little. If we need to cover our tracks.'

Gabriel was looking at her like she was the scariest thing he'd seen in ten years of life on the lam. The other kids were looking at her like she was . . . Sadie.

A moment later, Colin asked, 'You just blew up the SadieSeer 100, didn't you?'

And Sadie cried, 'For science!'

But April was inching closer to the SadieSeer and saying, 'Sadie, you're a genius!'

Sadie beamed. 'I know. I've been tested.'

PREPWORK MAKES PERFECT

And so it began – the watching and the waiting, the planning and the worrying.

They split into groups and took turns watching the mini mansion on the monitors and scouring Winterborne House for a lock that could have been anywhere or looked like anything. But their biggest job might have been keeping Smithers and Ms Nelson from becoming suspicious.

By the end of the first week, they'd searched the entire first floor except for Smithers's room and the butler's pantry (which wasn't technically Smithers's room, but try telling him that).

They'd looked in bathrooms and closets, behind suits of armour and under potted plants. They spent a whole rainy day scouring library shelves and a whole night going through row after row of fencing trophies and polo trophies and a spelling bee trophy that was placed right beside an Olympic medal that Gabriel's father had won before Gabriel was born.

But no little boxes. No chests. No drawers. No secret compartments. And absolutely no locks.

The good news was they still had a lot of places to look. The bad news was they had soooooo many places to look!

When they weren't looking for the lock, they were keeping an eye on Evert and trying to figure out how to resteal the key.

You might think that spying on a murderous, villainous, utterly evil uncle would be interesting. Well, April admitted later, you'd be wrong. If anything, Evert was boring.

Every morning he ate the same breakfast: oatmeal.

Every day he wore the same thing to work: a black three-piece suit.

Every night he went to bed at the same time: 10:45.

And when he was all alone – when he thought no one else was watching – he'd bring out April's key and hold it tight, just like she used to do. It made April feel sick. *And* it made her want to climb through the screen and claw his eyes out.

The good news was that they knew where the key was. The bad news was that it was on Evert. Like literally on him. Almost all the time. He wore it on a chain that he kept in his pocket, and he only took that off when he was sleeping. April wanted to break into his room with a knife – just to see how he liked it. But . . .

'He has bodyguards. Big, scary ones,' Colin said for what must have been the hundredth time a week after they'd first started their vigil.

Gabriel bristled and mumbled something that sounded like *they aren't that scary*, but April wasn't really listening. She'd heard it all before.

'How many guards on the perimeter?' Tim asked.

'Four,' Sadie said.

'We can handle four. Can't we?' April asked, but Sadie glanced nervously around.

'Plus dogs. I don't do dogs,' Colin said, but Tim just crossed his arms.

'I've got the dogs,' Tim said, and April kind of didn't want to know what he meant by that, so she didn't ask any questions.

'We could do an Avon Lady,' Colin said. 'That'll get us past the gates.'

'I don't know what that is,' Sadie admitted.

'For you we'd make it a Girl Scout. But he knows us. Darn it. Ooh! How about the Three Horned Dragon?' Sadie looked at him like he was crazy, so Colin rolled his eyes and said, 'Cons are in my blood, love. You've got to trust me. All we'd need is a hot-air balloon, a blowtorch, and three monkeys.'

'Colin—'

'OK, Sade. Two monkeys. Tops!'

'Colin!'

'One monkey and a larger-than-average ferret?'

'Enough!' Gabriel snapped. 'Go to bed.'

'It's seven o'clock,' Colin complained, and April couldn't exactly blame him. She didn't want to go to bed, either. She wanted to steal her key back and find the lock. And she was just starting to say so when something on the monitors caught her eye because, for once, Evert was doing something different.

She got up and eased closer to the screens. She didn't even realise Gabriel was behind her until he said, 'It's poker night.' On the screens, Evert sat around a table with five other men. There was a deck of cards and stacks of chips. 'He plays every month. Has for years.' Then he looked at

April. 'You're not the only one who does homework.'

She heard a banging sound on the far side of the cellar and heard Colin say, 'Ooh, where does this go?'

He was reaching for the old-fashioned key in the lock of a wrought-iron gate when Gabriel snapped, 'That's the old wine cellar, and it's dangerous. Stay out of there.' Gabriel glared and started after Colin, but April was stepping closer to the screens, and Gabriel didn't dare leave her alone.

'Who are they?' April asked.

There was the creak of an old gate swinging open, and soon Colin was shouting, 'Ooh! More swords!'

Gabriel winced, but he pointed at the man on the screen to Evert's right, then went around the table. 'Chief of police. District attorney. Mayor. Federal judge. United States senator. My uncle has cultivated powerful relationships, April. Power protects power.'

'You're more powerful than all of them. You're Gabriel Winterborne.'

'Am I?' He gave her the saddest smile that she had ever seen. 'Sometimes I can't remember.'

On the other side of the room, there was the clang and scrape of steel against steel.

'*En garde!*' Colin said, while Tim barked. 'Be careful!' but April kept her eyes on Gabriel.

'People still talk about you,' she tried to explain. 'They want to know where you went. And why. And—'

'You're doing that wrong,' Gabriel tossed over his shoulder at the boys, but he never stopped looking at the men who sat around his uncle's table.

'People would listen to you. They may be powerful—' She glanced at the men on the monitor. 'But you're famous. And rich. And you have friends, too.'

Gabriel looked at her like he didn't know whether to laugh or cry. In the end, he just snapped, 'You're doing that wrong!' again, then stalked towards Tim and snatched the sword away.

He stood there for a long time, considering, before he asked, 'Do you want to win fencing matches, or do you want to win fights?'

Tim smirked. 'What do you think?'

'OK.' Gabriel smiled. 'Then hold it like this.'

BIRTHDAYS

April couldn't see the sea, but she could hear it in the waves crashing against the rocks. She could smell it in the salt on the breeze. But, most of all, April could feel it in the chill against her arms and the way her hair wanted to curl. It wasn't raining, but she could tell a storm was coming. Sometimes, way off in the distance, the clouds would flicker and flash, and April knew it wouldn't be long until she heard the thunder.

Out on the water, boats passed up and down like they'd been doing for days, moving steadily back and forth. Like a grid. Like—

'They're still looking for him.'

April couldn't really see Tim through the darkness, but she could imagine the brooding look in his eye. Over the past week, he'd started to morph into Mini Gabriel. He was two swords and a thick beard away from going full-on alpha dude, and April didn't want to hear it. One full-size Gabriel Winterborne was more than enough, thank you very much.

'Evert knows he's back. He's hoping Gabriel died out there that night. But he'll be ready. Just in case.'

'So?' April said. 'We'll be ready too.'

But Tim just stood there, hands in his pockets. Wind in his hair. He didn't face her when he said, 'He's pretty good with those swords.'

'He used to take fencing lessons when he was a kid.'

'What he can do he didn't learn as a kid.'

'Yeah. Well. It's been his hobby for his whole life. I'm sure—'

'You need to ask him why he came back,' Tim cut her off.

'He came back to prove who his uncle is – which we will. We just have to get my key and find the lock, and . . . What?'

'He didn't come back to get a key he didn't know you had.' Tim was looking at her the way he looked at Violet sometimes – like she was too young and too naive to understand the world, and so he was going to protect her from it. Even if it killed him.

'Sure he did. He's helping us figure out how to get the key and find the lock.'

'Is he?' Tim asked. 'Or is he keeping us busy while he gets his strength back?'

'Of course he needs to get his strength back if we're going to steal the key! He has to . . .'

April looked back at Winterborne House while, out at sea, the lightning got closer and the wind blew hard enough to make her feel like she might fly away like a kite without a string.

'You need to ask him, April. Ask him why he really came back before you go fooling yourself into thinking that key opens up a happy ending.'

And then Tim was gone, back into the mansion and whatever it was that jerk boys did after saying jerk things to perfectly nice girls whose only crime was believing that everything might turn out OK.

But the worst part was the little voice inside of April, whispering that he might be right.

★ ★ ★

Winterborne House wasn't haunted. April was positive. Almost. The only ghost she'd seen was the man in the cellar, and he wasn't going anywhere. Yet. But as she crept through the dark halls, she heard the laughter of children. She watched pale lights dance and flicker across the floor. And she heard a boy's voice, shouting in the distance, yelling, 'Come on, Izzy! Catch me if you can!'

When she reached the door of the home cinema, she didn't go inside. She just stood there, looking in at Ms Nelson, who sat curled up on one of the big, soft chairs. There was a blanket over her lap, but those two mismatched, hand-knitted slippers peeked out from underneath, and she didn't even turn around when she said, 'You should be in bed, April.'

'I know. I'm sorry. I . . .' April trailed off as, on the screen, a boy-size Gabriel laughed and chased after a girl-size Isabella.

Ms Nelson must have sensed April's confusion because she said, 'I was raised here. Did I ever tell you that? My father was Gabriel's head of security.'

On the screen the picture changed, and April stood frozen, watching Smithers carry a cake with eleven candles and set it in front of Gabriel while everybody sang.

'It's his birthday,' Ms Nelson said. 'Or it will be. Tomorrow. He disappeared on his birthday.'

I know. He told me.

'Ten years sounds like a long time, but it's not. That's the weird part. It feels like just yesterday he was in this house.'

He's in this house right now.

Ms Nelson sighed. 'Ten years. I thought I had time.'

April couldn't keep herself from asking, 'Time for what?'

'Stopping Evert,' Ms Nelson whispered, and April knew she wasn't supposed to hear it. But she did. And it was all she could do not to shout, *We're gonna stop Evert too!*

But instead she asked, 'Stop him from doing what?'

Ms Nelson went still. She seemed to realise what she'd said. And done. So she blurted, 'It's nothing!'

'No. It's something. What's—'

'Evert is going to get a judge to declare Gabriel dead tomorrow morning. That's all. It's not a big deal.'

It is so totally a big deal.

On the screen, Little Gabriel was bowing to Little Izzy and then they were both pulling on face masks and brandishing child-size swords while a much younger Smithers and Sadie's father and a third man cheered from the sidelines and the two kids started to parry and jab.

'What happens then?' April asked, truly terrified of the answer.

Ms Nelson sat up and turned off the movie. She ejected a shiny disc, then put it in a cabinet with about a billion others, all neatly labelled with dates and names. April wondered what that would feel like – to have decades of family memories all safely stored and locked away. But April didn't even have a picture of her mother. She didn't even know her name.

'Ms Nelson?' April asked again. 'What happens when Gabriel Winterborne is dead? Legally.'

'Evert will inherit everything, and we'll move into a house that isn't old and draughty and full of mice. That's what will happen.' Her smile was bright. 'Don't worry about us, April. We'll be fine!'

Ms Nelson was a really, really, really good liar.

April didn't go to bed. She didn't even try. Instead, she found the little bundle she'd hidden away and went back down to a cellar that suddenly seemed too quiet.

She found him in the room he'd called a wine cellar, behind the metal gate, sharpening his swords.

He looked up when he heard her – took in her messy hair and sleepy eyes and the package she held in her hands, then snapped, 'Go to bed, April,' and pushed past her, into the big room.

He gave a quick glance up at the monitors, but April already knew what was there: guards and dogs and a killer safe in his bed. On the screen, the only movement was the ticking of the clock on the bedside table and the flutter of the draperies as wind blew through the open window, while Evert slept on, totally unaware of the storm that was coming.

'I mean it, April. Go to—'

'Here.'

Gabriel looked more than a little sceptical when she thrust a lumpy package into his hands, but that might have been because April had never wrapped a present before, and she hadn't wanted to ask Sadie for help.

'What's this?'

'Tomorrow's your birthday,' April said, suddenly nervous. 'I wanted to get you a gift. That's what people do, right? I mean, I've never had one, but . . . Whatever.

That's for you.'

He looked down at the package, but his voice sounded funny when he said, 'You've never had a birthday gift?'

April shook her head. 'No. Never had a birthday.' She shrugged because it wasn't that big a deal. 'I had a foster mum one time who said we should use the day I was found. But that's the day I was left, too, you know? So I'll just wait till my mum comes back. Then she'll tell me when it is.' She gestured to the package. 'Anyway, happy birthday.'

He didn't talk again as he tried to tear apart the old newspapers that April had taped around the bundle. She was just starting to wonder if maybe twenty pieces of tape might have been too much tape when he groaned and pulled a knife from his belt. He sliced, and the paper fell away, and then he stood there for a long time, looking down at what seemed to be a big pile of rags in his hands.

'Oh. Thank you. It's—'

'A coat!' April explained as he unfurled the bundle, cloth draping almost to the floor. 'We had to cut yours off, when you were . . . you know. About to die. So I thought you could use that.'

She'd sewn it herself out of a bunch of old coats she'd found in the master bedroom. They'd probably belonged to his father, once upon a time, but they were all full of tiny holes now and too small to fit Gabriel himself, so April cut them apart at the seams and sewed them back together until she'd made something that looked like it belonged on Frankenstein's monster. But the black and brown and green didn't look too terrible together. If anything, they blended into the shadows of the cellar. And it was warm. And heavy. April's fingers had hurt for days from forcing a needle through the dark, thick fabrics.

'You made me this?' he asked as he slipped it on. 'Did Smithers teach you?'

'No. I already knew how,' April said, sounding too defensive. 'Not all foster homes are awful, you know? Sometimes there are nice people who do crafts and rescue kittens and make soup. Sometimes they're OK. They just don't last.'

'I'm sorry,' he said eventually, breaking under the weight of so much awkward.

'It's OK. Nothing lasts.' She didn't know why she was suddenly snapping. Maybe because she wanted him to like the coat she'd made him. Or maybe because she wanted him to like her.

'It has a hood,' she added lamely, and he flipped it up, covering his dark hair and concealing his face. 'It's cold down here.'

'Thank you, April. No one has given me a gift in a very long time.'

He was rich, and April was poor. He was missing, and April knew that if she was gone too long, then Sadie would make a device that could track her anywhere within the mansion. But they were both orphans, she remembered. On that front, she and Gabriel Winterborne were exactly the same.

'Why did you go to Evert's house?' April didn't know where the question came from, but she didn't even try to hold it in. 'That night. When I saved your life—'

'You mean the night when you got me stabbed?' He raised an eyebrow, but April didn't take the bait.

'You were there because of my key, weren't you? I told you it was missing, so you went to get it back. Right?'

It should have been an easy question, but it took him a long time to say, 'I went there because of what you told me, yes.'

It was the way people talk when they're trying to lie and tell the truth at the same time, and April didn't like it. She didn't like it one bit.

'Why did you go? Really?'

'Because you told me someone broke into your room. With a knife.'

'So you *did* go to get the key?' April asked, afraid of the answer long before Gabriel started shaking his head.

'The key won't prove anything, April. And it won't stop him.'

'Sure, the key *itself* doesn't prove anything.' April wanted to roll her eyes. 'But once we have the key, we can find the lock and whatever it is he's so desperate to get his hands on, and then we'll get proof—'

'*There is no proof!*' He hadn't meant to shout. And he didn't want to cry. But he couldn't stop talking – April could tell. He had to get the words out before they finally dragged him under. 'The evidence is a boat at the bottom of the sea. The proof is a trail that's been cold for twenty years.'

'Then why did you even bother coming back?'

'I'm not back, April. I'm never coming back.'

'Look at where we're standing! You're in Winterborne

House. You're home!'

'This isn't my home.'

'Oh, it's not? Then where is your home, huh? Somewhere on the other side of the world? Some mountain or island. Fine. Go there. Live there. Be happy or whatever. But there are people who love you. There are people who miss you. There are people who have been waiting for ten years and maybe waiting gets a little bit harder every day, but they can't stop because if they stop waiting for you, then who are they, huh? What are they supposed to do then?'

April heard her voice quiver and crack. She felt the tears that burned her eyes and the snot that leaked out of her nose, but she didn't stop to think that maybe she wasn't just talking about Gabriel Winterborne any more. Maybe she wasn't talking about him at all.

'I think you came back because you don't want to be dead. I think you came back because running away is one thing, but staying gone for ever is another.' April took a step forward, and he took a step back. 'I think you came back because—'

'You're wrong,' he said.

'Then why did you come back right before Evert

declared you dead, huh? Why'd you come back *now?*' she asked again.

'Because I'm finally strong enough!' Gabriel snapped, but backed away. 'And he thought I really was dead until your little stunt on the dock. I had him. I was right there . . . I had him!'

'Gabriel, why did you come back now?'

'You know why, April.'

'Then say it. Say what you've been too chicken to—'

'*I came back to kill him!*'

April froze, waiting for the words to shock her or scare her, but she didn't feel anything for Gabriel Winterborne but pity.

'You don't have to do that.'

'I always had to kill him. That's the only way this ends.'

'Not if we find another way,' she pleaded.

'I won't—'

'Wasn't talking about you,' she cut him off.

She'd been walking as she talked. Inching closer and closer to him. And Gabriel Winterborne, being a big, tough guy and all, had been inching further and further back. He hadn't even noticed when he stepped into the wine cellar. Not until April reached for the metal gate.

He was fast. But not fast enough. And a split second later, the metal gate was slamming shut and April was turning the key and pulling it out of the lock. It was almost like the one she used to wear around her neck, she realised. Once she got hers back, she'd have a pair.

'April, let me out.'

'No.'

'April, you have to let me out of here. Right now.'

'Why?' she asked simply.

'Because . . .' he started but stammered, so April went ahead and said it for him.

'Your uncle left a window open.' She pointed at the monitors that showed Evert asleep in his bed, curtains billowing in the wind. It took a split second for Gabriel to smile.

'He did.' It was the first time April had ever seen him anything close to happy. And that, more than anything, made her sad.

Then she was walking towards the exit. And the cliffs. And the thing she probably shouldn't do but was going to do anyway.

'April, he hurts everyone!'

And for a moment, April stopped. She thought about

266

her friends. Sadie and her inventions and Violet and her drawings – Colin's jokes and Tim's secrets. Then she realised something else: she'd never had friends before.

It would be a shame to get them killed.

32

THE HEIST

April didn't remember her mother, and she had zero recollection of the day she was abandoned. Even the fire at the museum was mostly a blur, but as the rocks bit into her palms and the wind blew through her hair, April knew she'd always remember the night she inched closer and closer to the mini mansion. And the evil uncle. And the key that, according to Gabriel Winterborne, wouldn't solve anything at all.

But Evert obviously thought the key was important. So it had to *be* important. It just had to.

A flash of lightning filled the sky, and the wind smelled like rain, and April lay on her stomach for a long time, looking down on the mini mansion and waiting for the inevitable. She half expected to hear Gabriel's voice in her head – telling her she was making a mistake, that Evert was dangerous and April was a screw up. But the voice didn't come. Instead, all April heard was the sound of the wind and the thunder and the distant barking of dogs, which shouldn't have been a surprise, because, seriously, only one thing can come from strapping a whole package of perfectly cooked bacon to the SadieSeer 200 and flying it far away from where April lay waiting. Not all of the guards would go that way. But the dogs would.

And April was small. April was quick. April just had to watch the cameras and stick to the plan. Lightning flashed. Thunder boomed. And then she started to run. She stayed low to the ground, blending with the outcroppings of rocks until she reached the side of the house.

She tried to keep her mind on what mattered: the key. And survival. Even when the rough wood of the trellis bit into her hands, she kept scurrying up the wall like a spider, clinging to anything she could as she inched higher and higher. Even when her fingers slipped on the old boards, she saved herself because . . . well . . . April had always had to save herself.

And, eventually, she couldn't even hear the barking any more, so either the dogs had found the bacon or else the storm was just too loud. Or maybe it was the pounding of April's heart that made the whole world feel like the volume had been turned down – like it was some kind of dream as April reached the windowsill and slid inside.

They'd been watching Evert on the monitors for days, and it felt a little like déjà vu to stand in the house, just twenty or so feet away from his bed. And his bedside table. And the key that lay there, more tempting than anything April had ever seen in her life. This was the only time he ever took it off, and she wanted to grab it – grab it and run and not look back.

When the hardwood floor creaked beneath her feet, she froze. Lightning cracked. Thunder boomed. But the lump on the bed laid perfectly still.

Too still, April thought as a hot breath blew on the back of her neck and someone said, 'You're not quite the mouse I'd hoped to catch.' The light flicked on. 'But you'll do.'

April had thought Evert Winterborne couldn't possibly look any more evil, but, well, April was frequently wrong.

His eyes were too wide. And his smile was too big. And, really, no one should ever be that excited about catching an intruder. And yet he practically beamed as he glanced at the big beefy guard by the door.

'I told you no one can resist an open window.'

'Yes, sir,' the guard said, and April knew for certain it had been a trap. She looked at the bed.

'Pillows under the blankets?' she asked, mad at herself. She'd pulled that same trick a dozen times, and she shouldn't have fallen for it. She shouldn't have fallen for any of it! Her face turned red, but she didn't flinch when Evert crouched down as if to put himself on April's level. But April would never be on his level. No. April was better than him. And she knew it.

Especially when he said, 'Where is Gabriel Winterborne?'

He all but licked his lips, but April just shrugged and said, 'Dead. Thought you knew.'

Evert grabbed her arms and jerked her close. 'I know you've been helping him. I know he's back. And you're going to bring him to me.'

'I'm not doing anything for you.'

'Oh, but you don't have to do a thing. He'll come for you. And when he does, I'll be ready.'

April didn't mean to laugh. Really, she didn't. It was just one of those times where her inside thoughts got mixed up with her outside actions and she couldn't help herself.

'What is it?' Evert snapped, shaking her. 'You think this is funny?'

She knew she was supposed to be afraid, but he didn't get it. He really didn't.

'Gabriel Winterborne doesn't care about me!' April watched Evert's eyes go wide, and she realised what she'd said – what she'd done. But it didn't matter, April decided, because he was right. 'Yeah. He's alive. And, yeah. He's coming. But it won't be to save me.' April stopped laughing. Suddenly, nothing was funny any more. '*It'll be to kill you.*'

And then there was a boom that was louder than thunder and a flash that was brighter than lightning.

And then the lights went out.

THE LAST WINTERBORNE STANDING

April had always been a better-than-average kicker. And biter. But she'd always considered biting the weapon of last resort and she had no desire to know what true evil tastes like.

So April kicked. And lunged. And pushed. And ran. She could hear the commotion behind her, two big men pinging off each other in the dark as April ducked beneath their grasps and darted to the bedside table.

She wanted to shout with relief when her hand touched the key, but there wasn't time, so she just grabbed it and bolted for the door.

'April?' She'd had her doubts when Sadie had demonstrated the tiny device, but the SadieSonic was as clear as a bell as Sadie spoke in April's ear.

'I thought it was just going to be a *little* explosion,' April whispered.

'It was!' Sadie sounded defensive. 'At first. Anyway, the generator will be kicking on in five. Four. Three.'

Two seconds later, there was a clicking sound and then the lights of the mini mansion flickered to life, but April was already through the door and running down the hall.

'I'm out,' she asked. 'Where now?'

'Take a right up ahead,' Sadie told her.

April turned and sprinted down a corridor that wasn't quite as wide or as long as the one that ran along the back side of Winterborne House, but there was the same row of windows overlooking the cliffs and the sea.

'How'm I doing, Sade?' she whispered as she ran.

'Keep going straight until—'

April threw open the door at the end of the hall, but it was just a closet. 'Not an option.'

'Wait. I've lost you,' Sadie said, and April could imagine her scrolling through the various cameras, trying to find the ones that covered this part of the house.

'Turn around,' Sadie said. 'OK. Behind you. No. Wait. In front of you about halfway down the hall, you're gonna come to a big set of double doors. Take them.'

April found the doors, then reached for the handles, but they didn't turn. She lowered her shoulder and tried to push, but the next thing April knew, she was on the ground, rolling and wincing in pain.

'April, look out!' There must have been a time delay on the SadieSonic because the warning came too late.

She tried to scramble back, but Evert was already grabbing her by the arms and jerking her to her feet. 'Where did you find that key? *Where is the treasure?*' he shouted, like it was the most obvious question in the world.

'Treasure?' she asked, because she just couldn't help herself. 'I don't know anything about any treasure.'

Rain started to fall as thunder boomed, and blinding white light streaked through the windows, like someone taking pictures in the dark. It showed every line on Evert Winterborne's face – his eyes full of fury and desperation and a kind of madness that April had never seen before.

'Where did you find it?' he roared, but April snapped.

'I didn't find it! My mum gave it to me!'

Then `he dropped her, and his next words were a whisper. '*Who are you?*'

April was a girl with no family and no name, no future and no past. But before she could utter a word, a voice sliced through the darkness, saying, 'She's our friend!'

The next flash of lighting showed Colin at one end of the hall and Tim at the other. What followed was a whirl of thunder and punches and kicks. And some hair pulling. And a little tripping. And maybe a tiny bit of biting, because desperate times really do call for desperate measures.

The next thing April knew, Colin was on Evert's back, clinging to him while Evert spun around and around, trying to free himself by centrifugal force alone.

Sadie was in their ears, snapping, 'Get out of there. Now!'

Tim was holding up his hands, saying, 'April!' and April didn't wait. She threw the key in his direction, and he plucked it out of the air.

Colin boxed Evert's ears and jumped from his back. 'Let's go!' he shouted, and April took off after them, down the long corridor past the paintings of dead Winterbornes. She could hear the heavy tread of Evert chasing after her, and she reached for a table, pulling it over, hoping to block the way, but she never did stop running.

Lightning flashed – too close – and the house went dark. Then there was a terrible, piercing sound in April's ear as the SadieSonic practically exploded – way too loud one moment and then way too quiet the next.

All she heard was a guttural, 'Got you!'

All she felt was the burning of her wrist.

All she knew was that Tim and Colin were gone. They probably didn't even know she wasn't right behind them.

She felt herself being tugged towards the windows and pressed up against the rain-streaked glass.

'You're not getting away that easy,' Evert growled, but for some reason, April laughed.

'I may be here, but your key's gone,' she told him. 'Tim's probably chucking it in the ocean right now.'

'No, he's not.' Evert shook his head. 'But that's no matter. There's something I want more. I'll even let you keep your precious key if you tell me one thing.' He pulled her close. 'Where is Gabriel Winterborne?'

Tim and Colin had the key. Tim and Colin were getting away, and April told herself that that was enough. It had to be enough.

'Where is—' Evert started again, but April was smiling. And saying, 'Behind you.'

And just like that, Evert dropped her and spun to face the shadows. Adults really are so gullible, April thought as she reached for the bust of some long-dead Winterborne and hurled it towards the long row of windows that ran the length of the room.

She heard the glass shatter. She felt the shards slicing into her skin and the rain blowing in her face as she lunged through the broken window and out on to the roof of the mansion's first floor. She heard Evert's cry as he realised he'd been tricked – that she was getting away. But April didn't dare slow down to gloat.

The roof was steep and slick, sloping out into the darkness and the rocks and the sea. But that only mattered if she fell. And April had no intention of falling.

She just had to get to the side of the mini mansion. Then she could drop to the ground. Then she could run back to Winterborne House and Smithers's soup and Ms Nelson's soft blankets.

Then she could go *home*.

'Come back here!' Evert shouted. Maybe he really was crazy, because he followed her on to the roof, lunging and sliding across the wet tiles and grabbing April's arm.

'Let. Me. Go!' she roared, but as he pulled her back, she made herself go limp. Then when he thought he had her, she threw her head back, jamming the back of her skull into his nose.

She heard him scream and felt his blood run down the back of her neck, warmer than the rain. But then he let go. Which should have been a good thing, but he released her with a shove that sent April sliding. And sliding.

And sliding.

Her hands were bleeding and raw, but she didn't even feel the pain as she grabbed hold of the gutter and held on for dear life, terror shooting through her as she dangled over the edge. She didn't want to look down. She didn't want to see the water crashing on the rocks below. She didn't want to think about the fall.

'April!'

At first, April thought the SadieSonic was back online, but the voice wasn't in her ear. No. The voice was on the wind, coming out of the night, too rough and too gravelly to belong to anyone else.

And there he was, standing on the highest point of the rooftop, the coat April made him billowing in the wind.

'It's you.' For a man who had been chasing ghosts for a decade, Evert Winterborne didn't seem especially happy to have found one.

'I hear you've been looking for me, Uncle.' Gabriel inched forward, and Evert inched back. 'Is this the part where I tell you to pick on someone your own size?' He pulled a sword out from beneath his coat with one hand and gripped a knife with the other, and he kept his gaze on Evert, even as he shouted, 'Stay perfectly still, April. This won't take long.'

But the gutter picked that moment to groan beneath April's weight. A screw broke loose, and the metal jerked, and April screamed.

Then there was a new voice, shouting, 'Gabriel! Your knife!' and April looked up to see Ms Nelson easing through the broken window and sliding across the rain-slicked tiles as the boy she used to spar with tossed his knife into the air. Lightning flickered off the polished blade as it landed in her outstretched palm – like some kind of trick they'd perfected decades ago that never did get rusty.

And then she twisted, driving the sharp blade into the roof, dragging it along until she came to a stop by April, anchored and sure.

'April, take my hand,' Ms Nelson said, but April was too frightened to even speak.

She regretted never learning how to climb the rope in gym class. She regretted ever going on that stupid field trip to that stupid museum. But mostly, April regretted wasting her life looking for a mother who, so far as April could tell, never, ever looked for her.

The gutter shook again, and Ms Nelson yelled, 'April, take my hand! Now!'

And then April let go of the gutter and reached for the only woman in her life who had ever reached back.

Ms Nelson's hand was warm and soft but strong and sure, and April vowed to never, ever let go, just as Ms Nelson said, 'On three, I need you to let go.'

'No!' April shouted, but Ms Nelson's knuckles were turning white. Her hand was starting to shake.

'There's a balcony below you. I'm going to swing you that direction. Then you've got to let go.'

'No!' April shouted. 'I can't.'

'April!' The shout cut through the air, and April glanced down to see the balcony doors flying open. Then Tim and Colin were looking up at her while Tim shouted, 'We'll catch you.' And the craziest thing was that April believed him.

April could hear shouting, fighting – grunts and curses, and she knew that Evert's goons must have shown up to take on Gabriel, but April had bigger problems.

The knife in Ms Nelson's hand jerked as one of the tiles

gave way. They both jolted, almost falling, and Ms Nelson said, 'On three.' She started swinging April gently as she spoke. 'One. Two. Now!'

For a moment, April was weightless. April was free. She felt like the Sentinel himself as she flew through the air and dropped lightly on to the balcony ten feet away.

'Got you,' Colin said as Tim's arms drew her in.

'I'm OK!' April cried, looking up at Ms Nelson's smiling face. 'Jump! We'll catch—'

But then a terrible cracking sound filled the air, and Ms Nelson wasn't smiling any more.

It seemed to happen in slow motion. And it seemed to happen all at once. April didn't know how that was possible. She just knew that one moment Ms Nelson was grinning down at her, and the next the roof tiles were sliding. Falling. And then Ms Nelson was just . . . gone – disappearing over the edge and into the night.

It felt like a mistake. Like a dream. Like they could just call time-out and do it all again. But there are no do-overs in real life. April knew that better than anyone. She couldn't even find her voice to scream before Gabriel was rushing to the edge of the roof and shouting, 'Izzy!'

He glanced at April, then back to the rocks and the

swirling water below. And she knew exactly what he was going to do.

'No!' she shouted, but he was gathering purchase, preparing to jump. 'The fall could kill you!'

The rain still fell and the lightning still crashed, but there was no mistaking the sound of heartbreak when he said, 'Only if it killed her first.'

And then he leapt out into the darkness, towards the sky and the rocks and the sea.

'Gabriel!' April screamed.

But absolutely no one screamed back.

The only sound was the roar of the wind and the cold, cruel laughter of Evert Winterborne as he perched on the rooftop, surveying all he'd won.

The last Winterborne standing.

BEFORE THE DAWN

Hands. There were hands clawing at April, dragging her away from the balcony's railing, propelling her down a short flight of stairs and out into the falling rain.

'Gabriel . . . We have to go help Gabriel,' April said, but she felt numb.

'Gabriel's gone,' Tim told her, but that didn't make any sense.

'Yeah. That's why we've got to go help him. We have to—'

She saw Smithers running across the garden, shouting, 'Children!'

'We have to go get Gabriel,' April told him. 'And Ms Nelson. We have to help—'

'We can't help them,' Smithers said. 'Not here. We have to . . .'

Smithers trailed off, and April followed his gaze to where Evert still stood on the rooftop, watching. He actually waved, and April remembered how there was one thing he wanted even more than the key. And now he had it.

Gabriel Winterborne was back.

And Gabriel Winterborne was gone.

So Smithers ushered them back to Winterborne House as Evert's laughter echoed on the wind.

'What happened?' Sadie asked as soon as they stepped through the doors.

She was sitting at the bottom of the stairs with Violet. 'The lightning knocked out the SadieSonic. I think it must have hit a phone mast, because *nothing* has a signal, and . . .' She looked around, trailing off. 'Where's Ms Nelson?'

No one answered, but Sadie kept looking around, as if Ms Nelson was going to walk through the doors and tell them all to go to bed. 'Where is she? Smithers? Where . . .'

She must have seen the truth in Smithers's eyes,

because when she said, 'April?' her voice cracked. April knew that was her cue to hug Sadie and tell her everything was going to be OK. But things weren't going to be OK. Sadie had already lost a mum and a grandma, and now yet another woman she loved wasn't coming home.

And it was all April's fault.

'Hello?' There was an old-fashioned phone on the entryway table. April had never paid it any attention before – she'd never even heard the landline ring – but Smithers was holding the receiver to his ear, and his voice got louder and louder with every word. 'Hello! I'd like to report a . . . Can you hear me?' The last was part shout, part literal cry for help, but then there was the crack of lightning. Thunder boomed, and the rain fell against the house like a flood.

Then his arm went limp and the receiver fell from his hand. 'It's dead.' Which was the worst possible word. Violet flew into Tim's arms, but everyone just stood there, watching the phone swing back and forth.

'I have to go get help,' Smithers said finally. 'I have to tell the police what happened. Not that they'll believe me. But we'll need . . . *divers*.'

His voice cracked, but he didn't cry. No one cried.

'I have to go get help,' Smithers said again. 'I have to tell the authorities what happened. I have to make them believe . . . They're never gonna believe.' Then he looked at the kids as if he'd forgotten for a moment that they even existed.

'Go,' Tim told him.

Smithers looked at him. 'I shouldn't leave you—'

'We've been left plenty of times, Smithers,' Tim reminded him. 'Besides, who are they gonna believe? The Winterborne family butler or the foster kids who robbed Evert's house tonight?'

April could tell by the look in Smithers's eyes he knew Tim had a point.

'I won't be long,' Smithers said, reaching for the keys to the car. 'I hope. Stay here. Lock the doors. I'll be back as soon as I can.'

And then he was gone.

'Gabriel will be back soon,' Violet said simply. 'He'll know what to do.'

But Gabriel wasn't coming back either. And that was April's fault too.

★ ★ ★

287

They ended up in the kitchen even though no one was hungry. But there was something about the smells and the warmth, the comfort of that old wooden table and the clean, shiny pans. Like at any moment Ms Nelson was going to come in and ask them why they weren't in bed.

'I heard a splash.' April reached for the cocoa Colin had made her, but cried, 'Ow!' a moment later. She'd forgotten about the broken glass.

'Let me look at that.' Tim turned April's hands over to study her bloody palms.

'I'll get the first aid kit.' Sadie went to the cabinet where Smithers kept those types of things, but April just sat there, numb.

She should go take a shower. Tim and Colin needed to put on something dry and warm. They all needed to . . .

What did they need to do?

She had no idea. She only knew one thing.

'When she fell, there was a splash, right? You heard it, didn't you?' She looked at Tim and Colin, but Colin couldn't meet her gaze and Tim just shook his head.

'It happened so fast,' Tim said.

'Well, there was a splash. So she hit the water. And if she hit the water, then he probably hit the water, and . . .'

288

But April didn't finish.

'At least we got this.' Colin dropped the key in the centre of the table. For ten long years, it had been April's prize possession, but now she couldn't even reach for it. She didn't want to touch it ever again.

'Throw it in the ocean,' she said.

'April!' Sadie gasped.

'Gabriel didn't want it,' April reminded them. 'He said it was stupid. He said it wouldn't help, and he was right. He was right, and I . . . I got him killed. And Ms Nelson. It's my fault. It's—'

'Hey,' Colin snapped. 'We all knew that window was probably a trap. And we all decided to go. And, well . . . we had to try something, didn't we?'

But April couldn't help thinking that Gabriel had been right. Everything would have been better if she'd never gone looking for him. Everything would have been better if she'd never come to Winterborne House at all.

Tim started picking glass out of April's palms with some tweezers, but she didn't feel the pain.

She heard the others talking, faint voices that floated through her mind.

'Maybe a jewellery box . . .'

'*I think we should start in the secret passageways . . .*'

'*We should ask Smithers when he—*'

'Treasure,' April blurted out.

'What?' Sadie turned to April.

'Evert asked where the treasure was. He thinks I know. He thinks that' – April pointed to the key – 'opens it. He thinks there's a treasure somewhere.'

'Like it's not enough he just inherited everything,' Sadie snapped in frustration.

'Gabriel didn't even care about it. All he wanted was. for the world to know who Evert really is. Gabriel didn't want that stupid key at all.'

'Evert wants it,' Colin said.

But April wasn't so sure any more. She huffed. 'He told me I could keep it if I just told him where Gabriel was,' she snapped in frustration, 'but everyone was just . . . staring at her. And it made her snap again, 'What?'

'OK,' Colin started slowly. 'So he wanted Gabriel more than the key, right?'

'Yes! That's what I've been saying.'

'But . . . what's he gonna want now?' The house seemed bigger and darker than ever before as Colin said, 'And what do you think he's gonna do to get it back?'

The truth settled down around them. Gabriel was gone. So was Ms Nelson. And who knew how long Smithers would be away? They were on their own.

'We don't even know what it opens!' Sadie snapped in frustration.

Violet was the one who said, 'He doesn't know that.'

THE SPARE

Everyone knew what happened to Evert Winterborne
— that he was a cherished son. An adored little
brother.

That when his father died, he was perfectly content to
live in the smaller house and take the smaller inheritance
and play a smaller role in the business. And the town. And
the world. And when tragedy struck, he was there, ready
and willing to step into his older brother's shoes and fill his
role for as long as needed.

After all, he had been born a prince and would do
anything to help his nephew become king.

Nobody knew the truth.

Two hours after his sole remaining relative finally fell
to his death, Evert strolled up to his ancestral home. For a

moment, he stood in the lightly falling rain, staring up at the tall, imposing doors and the big iron ring with which guests had been knocking for centuries. But Evert wasn't a guest – not any more and never again.

His nephew was dead. The woman was gone. And the only thing standing between Evert Winterborne and what was rightfully his was just on the other side of that door.

So he reached for the handle. And turned.

It wasn't even locked.

Poor Smithers must have been falling down on the job. He'd have to be let go, of course. And the orphans would have to be disposed of. One way or another. But they wouldn't ruin this – his return to Winterborne House, so Evert threw open the doors and stepped inside.

The house was always a bit dreary, and only one dim light burned overhead, but Evert had always felt at home in the darkness. The storm was almost over, and soon the sun would be up. In a few hours he would walk into court and proclaim to the world that Gabriel Winterborne was dead. He wouldn't even be lying.

There would be questions, Evert had no doubt. Smithers would try to make trouble. But Evert had a shattered window and a broken nose and the Winterborne name. All Smithers had was twenty years' worth of rumours and a houseful of children.

Evert was a Winterborne. No. Evert was *the* Winterborne. And it was past time for him to take what was his.

But then he heard the laughter – haunting and faint. It might have been the wind, but it was more like a ghost. Or a memory saying, '*Father! Father! Let me try!*'

Evert froze, because he knew that voice, and for a moment he wondered if this was all just a very bad dream.

A nightmare saying, '*Go away, Ev. You'll get hurt.*'

'*I can do it.*'

'*No, you can't. That's my sword. That's* the heir's *sword.*' His brother laughed. And the taunt that followed had an eerily familiar tune. '*I'm the heir, and you're the spare. I'm the heir, and you're the—*'

Evert closed his eyes and shook his head as his father snapped, '*Boys, enough!*'

Then the voices faded, and the halls echoed with laughter.

'*Gabriel!*' a girl cried. '*Gabriel! Catch me if you can!*'

He searched the foyer and the hallway. He threw open

the doors and rushed into the library, but more laughter rang out.

'*Izzy! Come on!*'

The sound was coming from behind him. He was certain.

Then he saw the light. It flickered in the foyer, bouncing off the front doors that he had, almost certainly, left open. He was just starting to wonder if there were ghosts when a voice said, 'You made a mistake.'

One more time, Evert spun, but this time it wasn't a mirage. A girl stood on the stairs. She was younger and smaller than the one who had caused all the trouble. She had black hair instead of red, and big brown eyes. She looked unafraid as she stood in the beam of flickering light that sliced through the dark air like a spotlight.

'You shouldn't have come here,' she warned while the laughter of the dead echoed all around her.

'And why's that?' he asked.

He expected her to talk of vengeance and justice or maybe even ghosts because that cursed laughter was still ringing through the halls.

But she just pointed overhead and said, 'Because of that.'

Evert craned back his head to look, just as something flew through the air towards him.

He tried to duck, but he was too late. He tried to run, but he was too slow. A half dozen copper pots were already zooming straight for his head.

He stumbled back just as a boy screamed, 'Now!' and instantly, Evert was jerked off of his feet. Ropes wrapped around his ankles. A net fell over his head. A complex set of pulleys and wires sent him flying into the air.

And then there was more laughter. Closer. Louder. And from children decidedly less dead.

For now.

'It's on, mates!' Colin said.

Violet darted into Tim's arms, and for a moment, they all froze at the top of the stairs as Evert fought and clawed and clamoured against the net and the ropes and the wires. He didn't seem to notice the label that said SadieMatic Eight. He didn't even growl. And something about that was scarier. The last Winterborne April had caught had always growled, but he was gone, so April looked at the man who was swinging back and forth, glaring at her and yelling, 'You!'

Instinctively, April's hand went to the key that was back around her neck, but it didn't feel at home there any more. It was no longer an idea for April. Not a symbol. Not a dream or a hope. No. It was a mission, and she couldn't let herself forget it as Evert stared at it – the key drawing him to her like a magnet.

'You're going to tell me where you got that key. And then you're going to take me to it.'

'Take you to what?' April asked, defiant.

'The treasure,' he said, and April wondered, not for the first time, if he really was crazy.

'What treasure?' Sadie didn't even try to hide her confusion. 'You're a bazillionaire now. Isn't that good enough?'

'No!' he snapped. His eyes were wild. 'The Winterborne fortune is one thing – I was always going to get a share of that. But the Winterborne *legacy* is priceless. They thought I didn't know about it, but I always heard them talking – whispering. About how it would belong to my brother. I know it's here. I know they kept it from me. And now it's going to be mine. Just as soon as you give me that key.'

'OK. I'd tell you to come and get it, but you appear to be a little . . . tied up.'

April started to laugh. But then she saw the knife.

She watched the SadieMatic Eight fall into pieces. She heard Evert fall – too hard – to the ground.

She heard Tim yell, 'Run!' And then she felt her friends

scatter, going in all directions. But April didn't dare stop or even slow down.

Not when she saw him slip on the loose runner and fall on the stairs. Not when she heard him trip on the dental floss that they'd stretched across the hall. She didn't ask questions or demand answers. She just ran as fast as she could, zooming down the hall and away from the chaos, through rooms and down corridors, crisscrossing her way through the giant mansion that had somehow started to feel like home.

April was home.

And for some reason, that made her run harder. Faster.

'Ha!' Evil Uncle Evert was breathless when he appeared before her, bolting out of a passageway.

'You didn't think you could outrun me, did you? You didn't think you could outsmart me? In *Winterborne House*?' He laughed. 'I've been wandering these halls far longer than you've been alive.'

The double doors to the balcony were standing open, and April bolted out into a rain that was now nothing more than a heavy mist. The sky was getting lighter in the east. Soon, Smithers would be back, April told herself. Soon, the police would be there. Soon, someone would care.

'I am Evert Winterborne! This is my house! I earned it!'

April took a step back. She was starting to shake. Her breath was coming hard, in a way that had nothing to do with her mad dash through the house.

'Yeah. *How* did you earn it?' she challenged, sounding far braver than she felt.

'You think it was easy to blow up my brother's yacht and have the world think it was an accident?' He actually scoffed when he said it, easing closer and closer as April backed up inch by inch.

'It didn't work though, did it? Gabriel lived!'

'He didn't have the good sense to die when I needed him to, no. And then he had to run away like the snivelling brat he was.'

'Gabriel Winterborne was a hero!' April shouted, remembering the figure in black who had swooped into a burning building and carried her out the other side.

'He's dead,' Evert said, like it was all that mattered. And maybe it was. 'Ironic, isn't it? No matter how many times I tried to kill him, he always lived. He just couldn't survive my trying to kill *you*.'

It hit April harder than she would have liked, the reminder that Gabriel had survived shipwrecks and stabbings and who knew how many other disasters, but knowing her had been enough to doom him.

'You're going to give me that key, April.'

'No,' she snapped.

'You're not in a position to bargain,' he told her, so April grabbed the key and jerked, breaking the thin chain, then holding it out over the railing.

'How about now?' she asked. 'Am I in a position now?'

But Evert just shook his head.

'This didn't end too well for you before, April. And he's not here to die for you a second time.'

'And now you're the last of the Winterbornes.'

'I am indeed.' He smiled like it was the best thing in the world, and something in that moment – in that gesture – made April want to cry. And then it just made her mad.

'You had a family. You had a brother and sister-in-law and nieces and nephews and . . . *You had a family!*' she shouted again, heart breaking, voice cracking. 'Why'd you do it? You didn't have to kill them.'

'Of course I had to kill them! And I'd do it all over again if I had to. They thought they could keep my family's legacy from me? Well, now it's mine! Or it will be as soon as I get that key.'

'Did you get it?' she shouted to the wind.

'Not yet,' he said. 'Give me that key!'

April actually smiled at him. 'I wasn't talking to you.'

He seemed to change in the blink of an eye. Or . . . well . . . the blink of a tiny red light.

She could see the moment he heard the subtle buzzing sound that filled the air as the SadieSeer 200 flew closer to them, the red light growing brighter and brighter the closer the little drone drew to where April and Evert stood.

'Kids are obsessed with technology,' April told him. 'Or haven't you heard? We have apps for everything. Games. Homework. Recording murder confessions . . .'

He stammered and stumbled back. 'That's not . . .'

'Recording us right now? Of course it is. Right, Sadie?' Then Sadie and Violet appeared down below, a laptop open in Sadie's arms and a tiny headset over her ears. Violet gave April a thumbs-up as Sadie yelled, 'Copy that! We got everything.'

'It's over,' April told him, but Evert was lunging towards her, knocking her to the ground.

April's head banged off of the hard stone. Her vision blurred. The key flew from her hand and skidded across the slick patio, and April flashed back to the museum. She almost felt the heat. She could almost smell the smoke. She wanted to cry out for Gabriel, but he wasn't coming. Not this time. Not ever again.

Then Evert pulled her to her feet, her back to his chest, a knife at her throat.

'I killed my brother and his entire family. Did you really think I wouldn't kill you too?'

'Hey!'

The word shouldn't have stopped him, but it did. Or maybe it was the sight of Colin standing on the stone ledge that circled the patio and overlooked the sea, the key dangling from his outstretched hand.

'You'll let her go, or I'll let *this* go. Think I can hit the water from here?' Colin asked. 'Bet I can.'

'Do it,' April said. 'Colin, throw it!'

'Uh . . . not how you get the crazy guy to drop the knife, love,' he said.

'Do it!' April shouted.

'Let her go.' Tim eased on to the patio. 'Then you can have your key back and a nice head start, what do you say?'

'Yeah,' Colin said. 'You're a Winterborne. You've got money. I bet you could live a real nice life on some island somewhere.' He smirked. 'Or the Alps.'

'Just drop the knife,' Tim reminded the man. 'You might even be able to outrun Gabriel Winterborne.'

'My nephew is dead,' Evert said with glee.

'No.' Tim shook his head. 'He's behind you.'

And then Evert laughed. 'I'm not going to fall for that—'

'Now,' someone said, and Colin turned, hurling the key out into the ocean.

Evert roared, 'No!' and April broke free. Then she was falling again, pushed to the ground as something hurtled towards Evert.

No. *Someone.*

And it was the most beautiful sight that April had ever seen. The mist stopped and the clouds parted and the sun broke through in the east, bathing Gabriel with its golden glow.

'You're alive,' she said as if he wasn't already aware of that fact.

'I'm hard to kill, or haven't you heard?' Gabriel actually laughed. But it was a joyless sound, and he never once took his gaze off of Evert. 'Hello, Uncle.'

Evert was looking around, as if expecting the cavalry to arrive at any moment.

'Your men aren't coming,' Gabriel said simply, answering the unasked question. 'My family's money was well spent, but my last decade was spent better.'

But Evert only scoffed. '*Your* family? You should thank me, you know?'

'Thank you for what?' Gabriel asked.

'Without me, you would have been the youngest. The spare's spare. I made you the heir, you ungrateful . . .'

'Tell me, Uncle, why did you do it? Was it just greed? Money? My father would have given you anything.'

'Why ask when I could *take everything!*' Evert shouted, and the words flew away on the wind. 'I heard him and Father talking. About the business. The house. The Winterborne *legacy* that they kept locked away and didn't dare share with me. I heard them! And now . . .' A new light filled his eyes. 'And now you'll never have it. Good. Without the key—'

'What? *This* key?' Colin did his best to sound innocent, but his eyes were pure mischief as he made a sort of wave and the key appeared in his palm again, as if by magic.

Evert lunged – fast. But Gabriel was faster. He swatted Evert back, sending him flying across the flagstone patio while Gabriel stalked closer.

April recognised the sound of the sword sliding free of its scabbard. She knew Gabriel's stance. His tone. His one goal in life.

And she shouted, 'Gabriel!' But he didn't turn around. 'Don't do it.'

'This man killed my family, April.'

'I know. And he'll go to jail for that.'

Evert was trying to push his way up, but Gabriel kicked him back down.

'This man ruined my life.'

'Your life's not over yet. Not by a long shot. You have people who care about you. You have Smithers! You have me. You have us!'

'Isabella's dead!'

And that was all that really mattered. He looked at April, as if all the best-laid plans in this world had boiled down to this one moment, and then he pushed them away. 'Go inside.'

'No,' April said.

'Tim, Colin, take her inside. Right now!'

'No! I won't let you become like him.'

'It's too late. I'm already like him.' He kept his gaze trained on the uncle who glared up at him, a malicious gleam in his eyes.

'Yes, I think you are,' Evert agreed, but he was wrong.

'You're nothing like him!' April shouted. 'You're not here to kill him. You're here to save us, remember? We're precocious.'

She meant to tease, to make him smile. But he never even looked away from Evert, so she reached for his arm. 'Let's go inside, Gabriel. Let's go wait for Smithers. Let's—'

'He won't kill me, April,' Evert said. 'He's a coward. Why else would he have run away and left Isabella all alone?'

'Not helping your case there, mate,' Colin muttered, and Gabriel pushed April aside.

'He'll get away with it. He always gets away with it.'

'Not this time,' Tim said. 'We have him confessing. We have everything.'

'It won't be enough.'

'Yes, it will.' Then there was a sound on the wind, faint but growing stronger. Sirens. Red and blue lights swirled across the water as boats raced towards the shore.

'He's not getting away. See?' She pointed to the police cars coming down the road. 'The world is coming.'

But then April heard what she'd said – what it meant.

The world was coming to Winterborne House, and to Gabriel, that was more terrifying than all the henchmen and bombs and murderous uncles in the world.

His hand started to shake. The blade of the sword trembled. A light sheen of sweat beaded on his brow.

Sadie and Violet ran through the patio doors, shouting, 'The cops are almost here!' Sadie sounded happy and relieved and like the worst day of their lives was finally over. But April wasn't looking at the madman on the ground any more. She was looking at the man with the sword and then at the lights swirling in the distance.

'Run,' April said before she could talk herself out of it. 'It's OK. We've got him. You can go now. We'll be OK.'

'What?' Sadie sounded confused, but Tim understood what she was saying.

'Yeah,' he said. 'Get out of here. Now. Before it's too late.'

Evert looked from the police boats to Gabriel to the cliffs, but there was no escape.

'We caught him,' Colin said, catching on. 'We have him on video confessing to murdering his entire family. It's over.'

'Gabriel,' April said, panic in her voice. 'Go.'

308

He looked at the man at his feet. Then at the sword in his hand. Then at the girl who was saying, 'If you don't want to be back . . . If you don't want to *be Gabriel Winterborne*, then go. Find that island or mountain or whatever. Go be happy. She'd want you to be happy.' April looked at Colin and Sadie, Tim and Violet. 'We'll be OK. We're always OK.'

But April had never been a very good liar. Her voice cracked, and her eyes burned as she shouted, 'Just go!'

'Police!' someone yelled inside the house. There were more sirens. And above it all, Smithers was shouting, 'Children! Children, where are you?'

April could hear people on the rocks below, and she looked back at her friends and Evert. But Gabriel Winterborne was already gone.

April didn't want to cry. She told herself she wouldn't even miss him. He ate her bacon and didn't laugh at her jokes and never took her seriously when she offered to braid his hair. She didn't need him. Not even a little bit. Not even at all.

So she wiped at her eyes and yelled, 'We're out here!'

Then there was the pounding of heavy footsteps, shouts and cries, and police officers swarming the grounds, shouting, 'Who's there?'

'We live . . .' Tim started, but then he seemed to realise the officers weren't looking at the five ragged orphans with a billionaire on the ground at their feet. No, the officers were looking *behind* them.

And then slowly – so slowly April might have thought it was a dream – someone emerged from the rocky outcropping at the edge of the cliffs – hands raised. No coat. No sword. No knife. Just the ragged beard and too-long hair of a man who had to think about the answer.

'I'm . . . I'm Gabriel Winterborne.'

THE LEGACY OF THE WINTERBORNES

Turns out, coming back from the dead is exhausting.

There are interviews and exams. Questions and concerns. And paperwork. So much paperwork. Not to mention the makeover sequences, which aren't nearly as fun as they look in the movies. Or maybe that was only true for Gabriel Winterborne.

'Do you think he's OK?' Sadie said as they lay on their stomachs looking down at the man who sat at the big table in the centre of the library's main floor. Every few minutes, Smithers would bring in a new stack of papers Gabriel didn't read or food Gabriel didn't eat, but then the doorbell would ring again and Smithers would have to go turn someone else away.

The man in the cellar was gone, replaced by a shell

that April no longer recognised. He didn't even growl any more.

'He growling yet?' Colin asked, dropping to lie beside Sadie. Tim and Violet joined April on her other side.

'No,' Sadie said. 'And it's weird. I miss the growling. And the beard.'

Violet giggled. 'I liked the beard. It made him look like a pirate.'

'Right?' Sadie said. 'The beard worked.'

'You do realise I can hear you?' he shouted, but didn't look up. 'This room echoes. For future reference.'

April didn't know whether she should laugh or apologise.

'Master Gabriel.' Smithers reappeared at the door. 'We've had a delivery, and——'

'I don't want any more files,' Gabriel snapped. 'So tell the police or the FBI or whoever else is digging around in my uncle's dirty laundry that I don't care how many skeletons they've turned up. I don't need copies of every warrant or subpoena or——'

'But, sir . . .' Smithers trailed off as people started streaming through the library's doors, carrying crates and wheeling dollies. Soon the room was full of boxes and

Gabriel was looking around like it was the worst kind of Christmas morning.

Which was too much for five kids to resist. In a flash, they were all up and rushing down the stairs and towards the giant boxes. Well, everyone except April.

She stood perfectly still for a long time, staring. Because those boxes seemed . . . familiar. She remembered clinging to one just like them as she kicked against the current. She remembered men carrying them to Evert's house in the middle of the night. April remembered . . .

The museum.

When Smithers put down the crowbar and pulled out the first of the paintings, April was hit by a wave of déjà vu. And regret. And a little bit of confusion mixed with smoke because April knew that painting. That painting was supposed to be a pile of ash.

'Hey, I know these!' Colin was saying, but he sounded as perplexed as April looked. 'I thought they were in the museum that April burned up.'

'I didn't burn it up on . . .' April started but trailed off when she saw Gabriel's face go white as he drew a piece of paper from one of the crates. His hand shook. And then the paper fluttered to the ground.

A moment later, Sadie screamed as she plucked it off the floor and shouted, 'Ms Nelson!'

'What's—' Colin started, but Sadie shushed him. And then she started to read.

Dear Gabriel,

Welcome home. I always knew you were alive. It just would have been nice if you'd bothered telling me <u>before</u> we both almost died, but, when it comes to you, I'm used to disappointment.

I was able to track these down. In case you were wondering, Evert had copies made, loaned those to the museum, then set it on fire to claim the insurance. Evidently, he had no idea we'd tagged the originals with GPS ages ago (not the sharpest knife in the drawer, your uncle).

Regardless, I thought I'd see them returned to you. Consider it my last act as the head of the Winterborne Foundation.

Good luck, G.

You're going to need it.

—Izzy

P.S. Please tell April the fire wasn't entirely her

fault. The whole place was a powder keg before she ever broke in.

P.P.S. With my resignation you will, of course, become the legal guardian of the children.

April looked at the paper and then replayed the words over and over and over in her mind. *Alive*. Ms Nelson was alive, and the guilt that had been weighing April down for days was lifted and she felt like she might float away.

'I told you she was alive!' Colin was shouting, and they were all dancing and screaming, but April wasn't watching the kids. She was watching the man who stood at the windows, looking out at the sea.

April wasn't sure what had made him so pale – word that Izzy was alive or that she wasn't coming back. Or maybe it was just the fact that he was now responsible for the kids who were whooping and hollering and scattering straw and packing peanuts all over the library.

'She'll come back,' April told him.

'No. If she wanted to be back, she would be. No one can make Izzy do something she doesn't want to do. We always had that in common.'

'She's just mad you stayed away. She'll get over it.'

'Will she?' He looked at her like he honestly wanted an answer.

'Sure. Yeah. Of course.'

But his smile was forced. Even without the beard, he was still handsome, but he wasn't *her* Gabriel. And she missed him.

'It's backwards.'

April heard the words, but she wasn't paying attention. Not really. Not until she felt the tugging on her sleeve and turned to see Violet pointing at the fireplace, saying, 'Look, April. It's backwards.'

Then April followed Violet's finger. By that time, April was used to the sight of the Winterborne crest. It was in spoons and on plates, embroidered on towels and woven into carpets. April half expected to see it on the toilet paper sometimes, but Violet was right, whoever had made the fireplace in the library had made a mistake. The distinctive WB of the crest was, in fact, backwards.

'Ooh, good eye, Vi,' Colin was saying, but April couldn't take her gaze off of the indentation in the stone.

Her hand went to the key that she still wore around her neck out of habit. It didn't burn any more. Or call to her. But something in the little backwards symbol drew her closer. And closer.

They'd been looking for a keyhole for weeks, but what if they were wrong? What if the key didn't go *in*? What if it went *on*?

Before April even realised she was doing it, she was holding her key to the crest and placing it over the impression in the stone.

It fit. Exactly.

Everyone froze.

'Probably a coincidence, right?' April asked, but her heart was beating faster. Her breath was coming harder. And then she felt an oh-so-subtle *click* as she pressed the key into the impression. She wasn't breathing at all when she was able to turn the key, spinning it around like the hands of a clock.

And then the floor began to move.

It was like one of Sadie's inventions had gone rogue and multiplied and maybe been dosed with some kind of radioactive tonic, because the stones near the fireplace were cascading, dropping, *click click click* down into the floor – like dominoes – forming a spiral staircase that descended into darkness. Except . . . it wasn't dark. Not for long.

Flash.

Flint brushed against steel and the smell of gas was strong as lights flickered on one after the other, filling the space with a warm yellow glow.

'Violet! You found it!' Colin blurted as they all looked at Gabriel's stunned face.

'Stay here,' Gabriel said, before stepping on to the first stone step. A moment later, he stopped. And spun. And stared down at the five kids who were following him. 'I thought I said stay there?'

'Oh, you did,' Colin told him. 'We just didn't listen.'

And after that, no one spoke again. No one dared. They just walked down and down and down, through cobwebs and dust, footsteps echoing on stone, until the air turned fresher and colder and April half expected to come out in the sea.

But it wasn't the sea. And it wasn't the cellar. It was more like a cave. Or a church. Or both.

'*Helloooo!*' Colin shouted, and the sound echoed, but he looked disappointed. 'This isn't much of a treasure if you ask me. But don't tell Evil Uncle Evert that if you visit him. Tell him you found a mountain of gold or diamonds. Or something better than . . .'

He pointed at the massive room full of mats and targets, dummies and ropes suspended from the ceiling. It was like what Gabriel had tried to make in the cellar, except bigger and better and older.

'What is this place?' Sadie craned her head back and looked around. 'Some kind of gym?'

'Then why keep it locked up down here all secret-like?' Colin asked as he picked up a wooden sword and whacked the head off an old dummy.

'I don't know,' Gabriel said, but something in his tone made April think he had his suspicions.

'Why was Evert willing to kill to find it?' Tim asked.

'I don't know!' Gabriel said again. 'I don't . . .'

But he trailed off when Violet threw open the doors of a huge armoire, revealing a black hat. And several swords. And an honest-to-goodness cape – but not the superhero kind. The antique kind. It reminded April of the clothes in the museum, but also of the guide's story and the Sentinel's statue. And the whispers of a dozen kids who had grown up hearing that, once upon a time, the Sentinel had been real.

'Gabriel . . .' April started slowly. 'If this is the secret your father and grandfather were keeping from Evert . . .'

'No.' He was already shaking his head, like it couldn't possibly be true.

But April was nodding right back. 'Think about it! They made you learn how to use a sword. They called it the family *legacy*, right? Isn't that what Evert was rambling about? He said there was the Winterborne fortune and then there was *this*.' She threw her arms out wide. 'Evert thought it was some kind of treasure because Evert's a greedy moron, but what if it wasn't? What if it's *more* than that?'

'What if it's what?' Sadie asked, and she didn't like not knowing the answer for once in her life. She didn't like it one bit.

But it was Violet who picked up the hat and said, 'It's the Sentinel.'

'The Sentinel's a myth,' Gabriel snapped. 'A legend.'

'No.' April shook her head and tossed a sword – which *should* have been dangerous, but Gabriel caught it and held it like a second limb. 'It's a Winterborne.'

Eventually, Colin stopped climbing on the ropes and Sadie and Violet stopped playing with the capes and everyone made their way upstairs. Smithers brought out the sparkling

320

apple juice and set up an old record player in the library, and April watched her friends singing and dancing because Isabella Nelson was alive and Evert Winterborne was in jail. Kids like them weren't very used to victories, so they made the most out of this one.

But Gabriel didn't dance. Or sing. Or eat or drink. He just drifted back to the windows, Ms Nelson's letter tucked in his pocket, right over his heart.

April told herself she shouldn't bother him. But there was something she needed to tell him even more.

'I never did say thank you. For saving me.'

'Well, one might say that makes us even.' Gabriel glared down at her, but there was a twinkle in his eye. 'Just don't do it again.'

'OK. I'm pretty sure I'm ahead anyway. I mean, I did pull you out of the water—'

'Which I wouldn't have been in without you.'

'And nursed you back to health—'

'Which wouldn't have been necessary if you hadn't gotten me stabbed.'

'And I was instrumental in making sure Evert will probably die in prison,' April teased. Then grew serious. 'But I owe you for the museum, so I guess we'll call it even.'

She didn't expect him to laugh or smile back. He was still Gabriel Winterborne, after all. But she wasn't ready for him to look so confused as he said, 'What about the museum?'

'You know, when you carried me out of the fire?' she said, like it was the most obvious thing in the world. 'So I guess that means I owed you first, but . . .' She trailed off when she saw his expression. 'What is it? What's wrong?'

'April, I wasn't at the museum.'

She thought she'd misunderstood him. But he must have misunderstood her. 'I know you weren't there during the day. I'm talking about that night. I would have died, you know? I was too busy looking for the key and the smoke was so thick, but then you were there and you found my key and carried me . . . What?'

'April, I haven't been to the museum in fifteen years. Whoever carried you out of the fire, it wasn't me.'

There were so few things that April knew for certain. Not her birthday or her mother's name or how she'd ended up with a key that unlocked the Winterborne family's greatest secret. But she'd known that Gabriel Winterborne had been there – that Gabriel had saved her. April had been *so certain*. But April had been wrong.

'If it wasn't you, who was it?'

Gabriel looked back at the windows that had become a mirror with the fall of night. Her friends were still dancing on the other side of the room, but Gabriel didn't smile or laugh. He just stared into the darkness and said, 'That is a *very* good question.'

No one noticed the breath that fogged the glass. No one heard the low laugh that filled the air. Not a single resident of Winterborne House saw the figure who was running along the cliffs, blending into the shadows and the night, disappearing into the darkness like the wind.

Acknowledgements

I'm sincerely grateful to all the people who helped make this book possible. The team at HMH has been phenomenal, and I can't imagine better champions, with a special thanks to Catherine Onder and Gabriella Abbate.

As always, I could not have done it without Kristin Nelson, literary agent extraordinaire.

I'm overwhelmingly grateful to my very kind, very wise, very patient friends who helped me talk it through a million times, especially Carrie Ryan, Sarah Rees Brennan, Jennifer Lynn Barnes, Rose Brock and Bob.

Special thanks to Shellie Rea, who keeps the real world running so I can focus on the fictional.

And, last but certainly not least, my family. Thank you and I love you.

Author photograph by Liz Ligon

ALLY CARTER

Ally writes books about spies and thieves … who happen to be teenagers. She is the *New York Times* bestselling author of *Heist Society, Uncommon Criminals* and the *Gallagher Girls* series.

She lives in the American Midwest where her life is either very ordinary or the best deep-cover legend ever. She'd tell you more, but … well … you know …

Follow Ally:

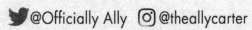 @Officially Ally 📷 @theallycarter